Intertwining of Time

*A Multi-Dimensional Story
of Love and Healing*

Dr. Neala Peake

Published by Synergy Press

Copyright 2010

Cover design by Christopher Panzer

Author's photo by Lynne Popkowski

BOOK ONE

B O O K   O N E

Chapter One

SHE WAS BORN several years past her fortieth birthday. Not born in the way most people think of it. She had done that in the traditional way forty-three years ago. In her second birth, she was born in the sense of finally coming alive - to her surroundings, to the people around her and, most importantly, to herself. What had she done during her first forty or so years? It was a question that was difficult for her to answer - after all, she had barely been there. To the outside world she had reached great heights of success. What people saw was a highly respected surgeon at a highly respected hospital. She lived in a highly respectable neighborhood, in a highly respectable high-rise apartment. The problem, however, was that she herself lacked respect for - well, just about everything.

She couldn't remember much of her childhood, but that was where most of it started. She had tried putting her hands over her ears, but her mom's shrill voice penetrated the fragile layers of skin and bone, as did her father's deep guttural raging responses. It didn't take her long to discover that trying to tune them out was not the answer. Books were. When she was engrossed in learning and studying, her parents' quarrels became meaningless background noise. Books were dependable. She never opened one to discover that it was drunk and incomprehensible. If it gave her a concrete fact, it would do so consistently, even if she returned to it months later. She loved books and concrete facts; it was people that she had little use for.

It was not surprising that she'd graduated valedictorian of her high school class, was at the top of her class in college, and graduated from medical school with honors. No one was surprised that she landed a prestigious residency in a prestigious hospital. But then again, to be totally honest, there was no one close enough to her to notice or be surprised by anything she did. She was only close to her books, and books were not known for their perceptiveness or ability to be surprised - which was yet another reason she liked them.

The change began in her forty-first year. She woke up one morning in her usual state of oblivion. She swept her wavy brown hair into a bun without any awareness of how thick and luxuriant it was, or how it framed her soft face when left down but gave her a hard, severe look when she put it up. It never occurred to her to wear clothes that might show off her long shapely legs instead of emphasizing the extra pounds she carried. She had no idea that on the rare occasions when she relaxed the tension she habitually carried, she could move with a sinuous grace. She failed to notice that the sun was shining for the first time in weeks, or that the doorman looked sad and was worried about his sick wife. But then she didn't even know he had a wife - nor did she wonder about such things. She arrived at the hospital an hour early. There was nothing unusual about that. She loved the hospital. Despite being aware that people died in hospitals - sometimes even people she treated and was responsible for - here everything made sense. Here everything was ruled by knowledge and facts that she understood. Here she felt safe.

As usual, her assistant greeted her with a cheery hello, which she barely noticed. Tasks remained to be done and people were there for the purpose of getting them done. She had no time for noting adjectives such as "cheerful" assistants or "depressed" doormen.

"So, how is the bypass recovering?" she asked, studying her notes.

"Oh, you mean Mrs. Johnson? Mrs. Johnson is doing quite well, and is in much less pain and better spirits today." Sandra paused, waiting for Dr. Pearson's impatient stare. As soon as she got it, she progressed to what the doctor really wanted to hear. "The patient's recovery is proceeding as expected, and her vital signs are excellent. Temperature 99 degrees, pulse 80, respiration 18, blood pressure 120/80."

"Very good. And still no donor for the congestive heart failure?"

Sandra sighed and shook her head, refusing to give up. "Oh, you must mean Jeffrey Davies. He's a really delightful man, you know. You should take some time to talk with him. His uplifting outlook on life has such a cheerful effect on those around him and I suspect his attitude keeps him healthier while waiting for a new heart." This time Dr. Pearson's impatient stare was paired with impatient foot tapping and a nervous fluttering of her pen on the patient's chart.

"I take all that to mean a simple no, as in 'No, Doctor, we don't yet have a donor.' Can we please now stay focused and get through the rest of these charts?"

Sandra sighed and for the umpteenth time wondered if she were wasting her time trying to change the doctor's attitude. She loved the opportunity to be involved with and to make a difference in people's lives. She refused to think of patients as only conditions or diseases. She shook her head one more time and proceeded to help Dr. Pearson with the "charts."

Neither of them knew that today would be the day the change would begin…

Chapter Two

HE WAS NOT a particularly impressive-looking man, but then hospital garb seemed magically imbued with the ability to suck out individuality and reduce even the most charismatic leaders of mankind to the appearance of inconsequentiality. She was not aware of the subtle aura of peace that emanated from "the newly arrived heart attack," as she labeled him in her mind. Members of the staff, without understanding why, kept gravitating to his room - finding all manner of reasons to attend to him.

Dr. Pearson allowed herself to be aware only of his medical condition and treatment - not of the man or his "presence." He tried making conversation with her and succeeded only in grating on her nerves. If she were to be totally honest, she found it much easier to deal with unconscious patients. Though it meant they were sicker, it allowed her to dwell on what was important to her: facts, diagnoses and treatment plans. This newest arrival was irritatingly persistent. He obviously had no respect for her training - not her professional training, but rather her finely honed skill of tuning out the human element around her.

"You're really quite amazing, you know," he said.

That comment stirred just enough curiosity for her to momentarily lift her focus from the chart and glance toward his eyes. The twinkle there only irritated her further.

"You aren't even going to ask me why?" he persisted.

"I will, if it will stop your chattering," she muttered.

"OK then," he responded.

"OK then what?" Her pen lifted off the chart for a brief moment.

"OK then. Ask."

"Ask what?" She sounded a bit irritated.

"Ask me why," he said with a gentle laugh.

"Why what?" Her irritation increased.

"Have you forgotten so quickly?" His tone was light and bantering. "I said you were quite amazing and then inquired if you were going to ask me why I thought so, and you said you would."

She put the chart down. "I have very little time and you are very sick and need treatment. Now, would you like to have a ridiculous conversation or would you like me to treat you?"

"Oh, but you *are* treating me." Again, the infectious laugh. "Treating me like one of those precious facts you seem so attached to." The lilting warmth that accompanied his words kept them from being offensive. "I'm not dead yet, so why not treat me like a flesh-and-blood man with a beating heart? It might even be the most effective treatment you could give me. My heart is pretty damaged and may not last much longer, but my soul has still got quite a spark. As long as it does, I intend to make the best of it." He paused. "So, what I was saying is that I don't get you - and I find that interesting. The point of your existence is treating people's hearts, and yet your own is completely blocked and essentially nonfunctional. An interesting puzzle."

She wanted to be angry and offended, but felt oddly curious instead. She took the time to make eye contact - an extremely rare behavior for her. For a moment, her imagination took off and she imagined him as some beloved Wise Man - a leader of his people.

"There now. Isn't that better?" He felt his own consciousness opening and expanding, and he stepped aside to allow it to happen. His eyes took on a faraway look. "There's so much you've forgotten. There was a time when you were open to everything, but this cycle you have chosen another path." He laughed his silvery laugh - softening his next statement. "You always had trouble understanding people who lived with a narrow view of life. Yes, sometimes the best way to learn is to become what you don't understand. Your parents were surprisingly good teachers. When you were young they taught you to shut down, be blind, and keep everything out. Thus they gave you the opportunity of having to learn how to open your heart and accept the world around you with compassion and non-judgment. Don't be angry with them. They did love you, even if they didn't know how to show it. In their own way they even loved each other - though it didn't seem like it when they fought so fiercely. You see, your mother always wanted more than she had, and your father was afraid of opening and giving. Their constant fighting scared you and you reacted by trying to shut out everything and everyone around you."

Dr. Pearson clutched the chart, using it as a barricade against the sea of feelings that were threatening to burst through. "How do you know that?"

Pulling herself together with an effort of control, she retreated to the safety of her role as doctor. She changed her demeanor and with it the direction of the conversation.

"What are you carrying on about? Perhaps we need a psych consult here? Do you know where you are and who I am? Do you know what day this is?"

"Oh, I know who you are, all right - who you *really* are," he continued softly. "There was a time when you would have looked into my eyes and remembered it all. Dear Nadjia, you have strayed too far from yourself. Look within. Remember what you have forgotten." His voice had taken on an almost hypnotic quality. "I can see it in you. It is still there. You can find it again. It's really so simple; you have only to remember."

"How do you know my middle name? I've never told anyone. And it's Nadia, not Nadjia." She felt something stirring deep within her and it terrified her. For a moment she just stared at him, then turned abruptly and left the room.

—⟋⟍—

Dr. Alicia Nadia Pearson had built herself a comfortable fortress filled with rules and certainties. There was no room in it for the unexplainable or the unpredictable. How did this patient know things about her and about her past? This didn't fit her sense of the orderly way the world functioned. She had seen the patient's name on the chart and could still remember it. She made a point of not knowing patients' names, yet having seen the "newly arrived heart attack's" name, she was disturbed that it had stuck with her. She tried to keep the knowledge out of her awareness, but it kept intruding. If he had a name, it made him real. If he was real, she had to deal with him. She could cope with the "newly arrived heart attack"; she had no idea how to deal with Douglas Fairway. She tried to convince herself that he was just a strange, possibly demented man, but deep within she knew that this man was far from crazy. Somehow, in one short meeting, he had managed to touch a vulnerable place deep within her psyche, cracking her well-constructed armor.

For the first time in her memory, she left the hospital as soon as her shift ended. She went home and wandered around her apartment, becoming aware of it in new ways. Before, it was important only as the place she inhabited when not at work. Now, she realized that it was cold and nondescript. There was little of anything personal to "claim" it as hers. Perhaps Douglas was right. She was a heart doctor without a heart of her own. The thought disturbed her, and the fact that it seemed to matter was even more disturbing. Long-buried emotions were starting to clamor for her attention. She was not prepared to cope with them. Exhausted and longing to escape her new awareness, she tried retreating into sleep. The next several hours were spent tossing and turning. When sleep finally arrived, it brought vivid dreams rather than oblivion.

When the alarm went off, she was groggy, out of sorts, and eager to return to her routine in the hospital. How had this one patient managed to affect her so profoundly? She decided to refer Douglas to another physician and have no further contact with him. It upset her when she realized that she couldn't even think of him now as the "newly arrived heart attack." Well, she would just bury any thoughts of him and go on with her life - that was something she was very capable of doing. Having made this decision she felt much better.

Chapter Three

EMOTIONS HAVE A WILL and a life of their own, separate from one's conscious thoughts and motives. Having been liberated from their long imprisonment, Alicia's emotions defied her attempts to re-incarcerate them. Her newly developing perceptions betrayed her desire to stay immune to life, putting her at war with herself. She discovered - much to her discomfort - that her assistant was more than just a convenience to help her with certain tasks. Sandra was, in fact, a pleasant and intelligent young woman who had an amiable way with patients. It pained her to realize that while she, as their doctor, left her patients with a reduction in the severity of their symptoms, Sandra left them with a smile. She tried rationalizing that what she did was by far the more important skill. However, despite her best intentions to ignore it, the fact remained that happier people with more positive attitudes healed faster. Statistically, they also returned to the hospital less often and were more amenable to following their treatment plans.

She may have put Douglas out of her life, but she couldn't shake his residual effects. Like a strangely reverse life-affirming cancer, these effects kept growing and encroaching on more and more "dead" areas of her psyche. As they did so, her dreams became more and more vivid. Despite herself, she began to awaken with dream images clearly remembered. Many depicted complex and rich lives in unique settings. She didn't know where these images were coming from, but they impacted her deeply. She could relate to these dream stories in an intimate way that made her uncomfortable.

Changes were also occurring between her and other people. At first she thought the other doctors and nurses were reaching out to her more, but then she realized that the change was in herself - not them. Her co-workers invited her to join them for a drink after work. Was this the first time they had done so, or just the first time she acknowledged them inviting her? She honestly couldn't answer. She accepted, and surprised herself by finding pleasure in sharing the day's experiences with others.

She had always been an excellent doctor; now she was becoming a more compassionate one. She discovered satisfaction in helping people, not just relieving symptoms. But still she felt at odds with herself. Emotions confused her; people scared her. She felt safe only when isolated and defended against the capricious inconsistencies of people's emotional states. Though she was changing by leaps and bounds and relating more fully to the world around her, she still allowed no one to enter the as yet uncharted realm of deep friendship.

One evening over drinks with her co-workers, she casually mentioned Douglas Fairway and asked if anyone remembered him or knew what had happened to him. A lively discussion ensued. It seemed that this genial older man - as many people referred to him - had touched many lives. They all remembered him and all had stories to relate. It was now six months after his discharge and no one had heard anything since. She supposed that was good. Hopefully, he was in good health and off doing whatever it was he did. No one seemed to know much about him personally. It appeared that most of his time had been spent relating to the people around him, with very little focus on himself. She remembered his comment about her heart being blocked and thought about the irony that this strange man with the big, warm, open heart was the patient, while she was healthy. Though she realized that it was his effect on her that had started the chain reaction within her psyche, she managed to refrain from thinking about the particulars. He seemed to know things he had no right to know, and his effect seemed almost mystical. This was something she was not willing to contemplate. She carefully labeled him as an odd, charismatic individual with the ability to make people more aware of themselves. She refused to explore why or how.

As the holiday season approached, she discovered yet more changes in her life. As a loner and an only child whose parents were long since deceased, she "celebrated" - if that was the proper word to use - the holidays alone. In her world, holidays were her time to catch up on the latest research so she could stay on the cutting edge of medicine. But this year she celebrated with her co-workers and lost count of the parties she was invited to. Like the proverbial stone thrown into a pond, each change had a ripple effect. She was slowly awakening from her long hibernation.

In January Douglas was readmitted to the hospital for what turned out to be a very mild heart attack. Alicia heard about it from staff and knew that he was scheduled for discharge that afternoon. She gathered her courage and decided to visit him before he left. She found it amusing that the thought of seeing him scared her.

She entered his room without the protection of a chart to hide behind, merely walking in and saying hello. He looked up and smiled his special smile that warmed the room.

"So, you've lost enough of your fear of me to pay a visit." It was a statement, not a question. "I'm quite delighted, you know. Always good to see old friends, yes?" She had forgotten how his laughter was like quicksilver, appearing at unexpected times and lighting up his surroundings. "You know, in some ways, perhaps I too am a heart doctor. If you were my patient, I would say you're doing well - quite an improvement. Yes, this patient may yet live. Besides, the world isn't really such a bad place to live in once you give it a chance, is it?"

She found his twinkling eyes disconcerting and

looked away as she spoke. "How do you know these things? I've only just walked in and said hello."

"How do you know I have gray hair, or that my nose is rather large and has a rounded tip?" he countered.

"Well, I can see that by looking at you."

"And there you have it."

"Have what?" She had forgotten how confused she could feel when talking to him.

"Your answer, of course. I see what I see by looking at you too. I just have better eyesight. You see only what's in front of you - only what you expect to see. My dear, there is a world all around us, if you would only open your eyes and your heart to it. You still have the ability to see it. You've just shut it down this time around."

"You confuse me. I never know what you're talking about."

"Actually," he responded, "I don't confuse you. I scare you because you know exactly what I'm talking about. Who you are - in *this* here and now - is only a small part of you. You accept that to a degree when you acknowledge the existence of emotional aspects of yourself you have disconnected from. There is so much more to all of us than meets the physical eye."

"What do you mean by 'this' here and now? What are you implying?"

"What do you think I'm implying?"

"I sincerely hope that you aren't suggesting you believe in reincarnation?"

Again the silvery laugh. "Why do you think those dream images of yours are so tantalizingly familiar and so vivid? You have the ability to connect to the many and varied aspects of your soul."

"How do you know what I dream? None of this makes any kind of sense. And on top of that, I certainly can't and won't entertain the idea that my dreams are memories of past lives. Besides which, I don't even believe in the premise of past lives."

"That's because the premise would be inaccurate," he said a little more seriously, "though I must admit it would be a much easier starting point. You assume we live in a linear, three-dimensional world - and it does appear that way to our limited perception. But, just for a moment, suspend that belief and assume that the universe is ever so much richer and multi-dimensional than we can fully comprehend while in physical form."

"I don't know what you mean. Sometimes nothing

you say makes sense."

"Exactly my point." Douglas smiled, completely unruffled by Alicia's comment. "It doesn't make sense if you look at it from your usual perspective. So, let's change perspectives. Imagine the world of a two-dimensional man made out of a flat piece of paper who lives in a world that - like himself - is entirely two-dimensional. He can understand and see length and width, but has no concept of depth. Now let's suppose a three-dimensional cube intersects his world. Our two-dimensional being would be incapable of conceptualizing that the cube has volume - in other words, an interior - because to him a cube could be perceived only as a two-dimensional i.e. flat square. We know and can see that the cube has six sides; he believes it has only one side with four edges. Aspects of reality exist that our two-dimensional man is incapable of allowing into his consciousness without blowing apart his entire world view. So how would you explain to him that there is volume within a three-dimensional cube? Hold that thought and let's switch to the concept of time. What if time is actually multidimensional? As with our two-dimensional being, isn't it possible that there are aspects of time we can't see or even imagine? Couldn't the soul have simultaneous incarnations in innumerable space-time locations? I know this is very confusing, but the point is that there may be other ways to conceptualize our world - especially from the soul's perspective."

He paused for a moment, watching the look of confusion swirling in her eyes, but also witnessing the deeper stirrings of awakening. He knew this was more than she could fully take in. But not knowing how much more time or how many more opportunities he might have, he continued. "Right now you're a doctor, just learning to open her heart, but in another dimension you're a beautiful young tribeswoman - a healer, learning to trust her faith and spiritual powers. And on the opposite end of the spectrum you're also a young boy murdered by slave traders. I could go on and on. All of these are part of you, each is as real as your identity as Dr. Pearson and every aspect of you is learning and growing and becoming steadily more whole. And as each one learns, so do the rest. For most of us, the effect is slight. But the more we progress, the stronger the ability for one aspect of our self to heal the others. Even at your level of awakening, you're having an easier time dealing with the emotional changes you're experiencing because the young tribeswoman - who is also a part of you - has already mastered that lesson. Other aspects of ourselves can even affect our health. You think it's your wonderful modern medicine that's keeping me alive, but there are factors involved that medicine has yet to understand."

Alicia felt dizzy and disoriented. There were too many implications she could not accept. She slammed shut her mind's door before the full impact of what she was realizing could take hold. With great effort, she pulled herself closed. In the past, it would not have been so difficult to repress unwanted thoughts. Still, her years of training held. Within moments, she was comfortably numb and able to close their discussion with banter. "You're the strangest man I've ever met. I think my first impulse to call for a psych evaluation was not that far off. Anyway, it was nice seeing you again - at least I think it was. I have to get back to work." As is often the case, truth gets spoken indirectly through humor. She laughed as she said: "Take care of that heart of yours so you don't have to return here. You're too much for me; I'm not sure I could handle seeing you again."

"Well, in case I don't get to see you again, I'll give

you one more thing to think about. I came here - to this hospital - partly because of you. You and I have a connection that's interwoven through other dimensions and between our other selves. You needed my help, and in a way you called me to give it to you. I hope I've done so." She appeared uncomfortable and he realized that she was not yet ready to understand or accept what he had just said. He hoped it would make sense as time progressed. Her response echoed his observation. She nodded briefly and quickly left the room.

—⚬—

Life continued becoming richer and fuller as Alicia allowed more aspects of herself free expression. She was grateful to Douglas for beginning the process of cracking open her shell. However, one aspect of their last meeting still disturbed her. It was his comment about her dreams. Sometime after her first meeting with Douglas, she began having dreams that were unusually vivid and powerful. They were different from anything she had ever experienced, and she could recall them all with remarkable clarity. He had spoken about these dreams as being other aspects of herself - what most people would term past lives - a concept she didn't even want to entertain. She had always dismissed such ideas as fanciful. If one believed that the soul incarnated over and over again, then death became less frightening, and the difficulties one encountered in life could be seen as having divine purpose. To her, these ideas were crutches used by the weak to cope with the more painful aspects of being human. Other people were welcome to believe whatever they needed to help them get through the day, but these ideas were not for her. Perhaps what disturbed her most was that this belief in other lives - particularly simultaneous other lives - implied that her entire construct of reality was defective, and she was not ready to give up the comfort of dependable facts and rules that never varied. For example, a person could have a heart attack. If the heart attack was not treated, they could die. This had nothing to do with other incarnations or other aspects of self. It had to do with the condition of the person's heart and medical treatment. Douglas had implied otherwise. While she tried to dismiss the implications, one fact of their conversation above all others made this particularly difficult. He had mentioned specific dreams - in particular, one about her being a young woman healer living in a tribe, and another about being a young boy who had been killed by slave traders. She had dreamt about both of these people more than once, and in great detail. Whatever the stories were, Douglas apparently knew the same stories, and that was simply not possible in her current conception of reality. She was not yet prepared to dismiss a lifetime of beliefs. She could accept the existence of repressed emotional aspects of herself and she could see the value of no longer disowning them, but she would not consider the possibility that there were aspects to reality that she could not observe, or that there were other aspects of her consciousness that somehow existed in an alternate time and space. While she had changed considerably and was much happier for it, she had come to the limits of how much change she could accommodate at this point in her life.

Chapter Four

TIME MOVED ON and the holiday season was once more approaching. Her life had changed so profoundly in a single year as to be almost unrecognizable. The biggest change occurred in March during a medical seminar. It was there, during a long-winded and sometimes heated panel discussion about the uses of various stress-reduction techniques on heart patients, that she had met Brian. He was gentle, a bit shy and made her feel comfortable and safe. Quickly discovering that they had much more in common than just their professions, they began to date. As their relationship progressed, Alicia felt that for the first time in her life, she was falling in love.

On December 30th they were driving home from a romantic dinner, discussing how they would spend New

Year's Eve and sharing plans for their next year together. Alicia was happier than she had ever thought possible. It was at this moment that fate chose to step in and alter the course of Alicia's life.

The oncoming car spun out of control and slammed into them, throwing their car off the road and down into a ditch. The seatbelt should have held -but it didn't. The door should have been strong enough to stay shut on impact, but it wasn't. Brian went flying out of the car, landing on the ground with enough force to break his right leg. A small sharp-edged piece of metal broke free from the car, flew through the air following Brian's path and hit him in the stomach, cutting him deeply. Despite his extreme pain, his first thought was for Alicia's condition. He was terrified that she was seriously injured and lying somewhere in pain because of a misjudgment on his part. Seeing the blood gushing from his stomach, fearing for Alicia's safety, and suffering great pain, he fainted. Alicia remained in the car, hit her head, and passed out. Fortunately, the passenger in the other car was conscious long enough to call for an ambulance.

The paramedics arrived on the scene relatively quickly and assessed everyone's condition. They stopped

Brian's bleeding and proceeded to immobilize his leg. They determined that his injuries were not life-threatening, but were concerned that he did not wake up. They rushed both Brian and Alicia to the hospital.

The doctors ran them through all the proper procedures and did everything within their medical training. They had no idea how often that training was woefully inadequate. One doctor, however, was beginning to learn…

—٨٨٨—

She saw the lights of the oncoming car and realized with horror that it was coming directly at them. It happened so fast that there was no time for thought as she felt the car hurtling down the steep ravine. Her next awareness was of Brian, his leg bent at an unnatural angle and blood streaming out of his stomach. She didn't realize that anything was amiss until she reached out to help him and discovered that she couldn't make physical contact with him. To her horror, she realized she was no longer in a physical body. Her first response was terror. There was only one possible interpretation. She must be dead. This was not how she had conceptualized death. For one thing, it seemed too similar to life. Except for being without her body, she still thought and felt emotions just as she always did. She wondered what had happened to her body, and immediately found herself hovering above her still form. That's when the shock set in. *This can't be happening. It can't. Not now! Not when I'm finally happy for the first time. If I'm dead, how can I be feeling so completely panic-stricken? It's just not fair! If this is death, it really sucks. I don't think I've ever in my life felt such terror! But then it appears that I am no longer 'in my life?'* She began to laugh hysterically and wondered if one could have a nervous breakdown after death.

From out of nowhere she felt a soothing vibration reach her. It was subtle and tenuous but helped her regain some measure of control. As the panic finally subsided, she took stock of her predicament. If she was dead, so be it. There was not much she could do about it, so she decided she might as well explore and see what could be learned. She made herself look at her own still form - this time without panicking. It was odd to look upon herself in such an objective way. She had never realized that she was actually kind of pretty. She supposed it was regrettable that she only saw that now.

She felt disappointed that death wasn't more exotic - no trips through tunnels, no angelic beings, beautiful white light or peace beyond imagining. Perhaps there was something else she needed to do before she could have all that. Her thoughts turned to Brian and immediately she was back at his side. Her perceptions were altered and expanded. She didn't need sophisticated medical equipment to know about Brian's condition. She could see more about his leg than any X-ray could show her. She knew how long it would take to heal and that there would be no residual problems from the break. She could see that the stomach wound was not deep enough to be life-threatening. She could also see that there was no medical reason for Brian to be unconscious. The accident and injuries had stirred a resonance buried deeply within his soul and his psyche. The effect was weakening his connection to his body. This realization shattered long-held beliefs.

As a doctor, she had seen many cases where patients died unexpectedly. Doctors learned to accept it. They were not omnipotent gods. Some people came back from the brink of death by what seemed a miracle, and others died of minor injuries. Now she was faced with the realization that the man she loved might die because of an echo of some experience held within his soul. Previously, these were the kind of thoughts she had purposely shied away from. Douglas had terrified her when he suggested the existence of other planes of existence. Now she was living in one. So much for a lifetime of clinging to facts she could verify with her mind and her five senses.

She watched as the paramedics worked on Brian and then loaded him and her inert body into the ambulance. She had been so focused on Brian that she had diverted no thoughts or concerns to herself. After all, if she was dead, there didn't seem to be anything she could do about it. So she was surprised when she heard the paramedic discussing her condition and realized that she was not yet dead. With this realization she became aware of a silver cord that came out of her physical body and connected her to her present form. She somehow understood that as long as that cord was intact, she was still alive. She started to feel a kinship with Alice in Wonderland. *Not so easy to have your world turned upside down, is it, girl? Sorry I wasn't more sympathetic to your plight when I first read about you.* Like Wonderland, everything in her world had become curious and absurd.

Chapter Five

BACK AT THE HOSPITAL, Alicia grew increasingly agitated. They kept poking and prodding Brian when the problem was clearly not with his physical self. Uncertain as to what to do, she wandered back to her own room and hovered over her body, watching from the upper right-hand corner of the room as a fascinating drama unfolded.

The young intern was looking intently at the attending physician "So, Dr. Grant, behind all this sophisticated medical jargon, all you're really saying is that she's unconscious, and we really don't know why. Furthermore, she may or may not wake up, and if she does we don't really know when. Makes you feel pretty helpless, doesn't it? Isn't there anything more we can do?"

"Maybe. Is Dr. Hardin in?"

"He's seeing the gentleman who was driving the car she was in. But really…You can't be thinking of bringing him in on this even if he does specialize in brain trauma and comas. I mean …well…perhaps he's just been here too long and needs to retire. I think maybe he's losing it a bit."

Dr. Grant smiled. "He's been here 35 years; I've worked with him for the past 30. He's always been a bit strange, but his track record of working with coma patients is beyond amazing. Don't question what you don't know. His reputation is well-earned." He looked meaningfully at Dr. Stern. "I mean his impressive medical reputation, not the petty gossip spread by the ignorant."

As soon as Dr. Hardin arrived, Alicia saw that he "looked" different from everybody else in the room. She wasn't quite sure how to describe it. She realized that each person has a "presence" as individual as their fingerprints, and his was much larger and brighter than everyone else's. As he entered the room, he glanced at the corner where Alicia was hovering. She wondered for a moment if he could see her. But, just as quickly, he averted his gaze and went directly to her physical body. He examined her, made notes, examined her some more, checked her chart, reviewed all the tests that had been done, did a few quick ones of his own, and then studied her once again. He became quiet and thoughtful. Looking away from the chart, he stared out into space. At least that's what it looked like to the other doctors.

To Alicia it looked altogether different. When he first examined her physically, she could feel his psyche probing her, looking for clues beyond the merely physical. When he looked away from the chart he was not staring off into empty space. He looked directly at her and began to speak. "Now, the young man who came in with her, he needs help and his condition is not stable. This one can come back on her own, but not the man. He'll need some help. You understand?" His eyes stayed focused on Alicia's disembodied form. "It's just a question of learning what must be done. If I didn't know what to do, personally I'd ask for assistance. Never know what kind of help is out there - if you know what I mean. No good trying to do it all alone, but sometimes people are afraid to ask for help. Yup, I know how this stuff works. Asking for help - that's the ticket." She wanted to ask him a question but wasn't sure how or what to ask. However, she was certain that his message was meant for her.

She could see the young intern losing patience. "Excuse me, Dr. Hardin, but what are you talking about?"

Dr. Hardin switched his gaze to the intern. "There is a lot we doctors don't know and a lot of questions we're unwilling to ask. There is no permanent damage here. It will take some time, but she'll recover. She'll find her way back."

"So what kind of help does she need?"

"Not the kind that young doctors who think they already have all the answers can give. Sometimes the answer isn't medical. She just needs time and some old-fashioned rest. Stop running tests, stop disturbing her." He looked directly at Alicia once again. "Mark my words, she'll be fine. She just has some things she needs to figure out." He returned his attention back to the intern. "Just ask Dr. Grant. I've never been wrong yet."

As she watched him leave the room, Alicia thought: *He wants me to help heal Brian, but I don't have the vaguest idea what to do. I don't have any training for this. In fact, I've spent years fighting against believing that any of this could possibly be real. I'm really out of my element here.* Catching the absurdity of that last comment, she added: *in more ways than one.*

She thought about Brian and found herself again by his side. *What am I to do? I don't understand. How am I supposed to help you?*

She thought back to the doctor's strange message to her. *Obviously, he wants me to ask for help and I certainly need it - so I guess I'll ask. But whom do I ask?* One phrase stood out from his message: "Never know what kind of help is out there - if you know what I mean." She was afraid she did know what he meant and didn't like the implications one bit. *OK, Alice, is this how you felt when you had to make choices in Wonderland? Let's see, would I rather see Brian die or ask for help from whatever scary things might be out here? How do I know I won't conjure up evil things that go bump in the night and traumatize bodiless - whatever it is I am - that find themselves hanging around here? I'd feel a lot safer if I could understand the rules here.*

All that Alicia had figured out thus far was that her thoughts were powerful. If she thought about her body, she found herself near it, and if she thought about Brian she immediately found herself by his side. Yet, when she thought about needing help, nothing happened - which was a relief since she was terrified of what might show up. She didn't really want something unknown helping her, yet the doctor had warned her about being afraid to ask for help.

"All right. I guess I'm ready. Is anyone - or anything - out here? I'm willing to ask for help. Just don't scare me too much, OK? I want to help Brian, but I'm already pretty freaked out. I don't know how much more I can take."

Immediately, she saw a glowing light moving toward her. As it came closer she realized that it was an angel with wings and a flowing white gown.

"Greetings, Alicia. You have asked for our help."

Her reply was not the respectful response she thought she would have upon seeing an angel, but she couldn't help herself. "You've got to be kidding! I can't believe this. I mean… Are you for real? Like, you guys really exist?"

The angel dissolved into an ancient Oriental man in a monk's robe and with wise kind eyes. "Does this form make you more comfortable? You did ask that our appearance not frighten you. Is there another form you would prefer?"

"No, I guess you've made your point. You can be whatever I want you to be, and if I'm frightened it's my own choice to feel so. This form is as good as any."

"We don't need to be in any form at all. We can speak directly to your consciousness, but we determined that doing so would make you uncomfortable. We will, therefore, remain in a form that appears separate from yourself. We are limited in what we are allowed to do. We have heard your request. We cannot heal Brian directly, nor can we impart knowledge to you directly. We can offer you assistance, but it will be up to you to make sense of it all. Listen carefully. Here is our gift to you. You sensed correctly. What is wrong with Brian is an echo from the past. Follow the echo and heal the wound. By doing so, you will heal yourself as well." The energy shifted and, as it did, a new and singular voice emerged.

"Right now, it's not possible for me to say or do more. However, I will be with you, helping and supporting you in every way I can. Don't be afraid. All will be well. Listen to the silence within for that is where I will be. Farewell. Remember, you are not alone."

Chapter Six

RETURNING TO BRIAN and hovering over him, she sensed his life force weakening. *Now, how do I know that?* she asked herself. The question brought back a snippet of a past conversation with Douglas. He had implied that he knew things because he saw in a nontraditional way. *OK, Brian, let's find out if I can "see" this echo I'm supposed to follow.* She had a sense that this decision was being met with approval and felt rather than heard the message to "look," but not directly with the eyes. Figuring that this made as much sense as anything else that had happened so far, she looked at Brian. Nothing happened. She tried looking at him without really focusing. Again, nothing happened. *How do I look without my eyes?* she mused. She surrendered and gave up trying to make it happen. Immediately, she began to see images floating around Brian's head.

Well, I'm seeing things, so either I've gone completely nuts or I'm on the right track. I sure hope it's the latter. Now what do I do?

Kaleidoscopic images floated above Brian's head giving the appearance of a constantly shifting, changing tangle of pictures and colors. She tried adjusting the images and bringing them into focus but without success; she switched to making adjustments within herself. She was starting to understand that she was the root cause of all that occurred. When she anxiously strived, nothing happened. Things worked when she calmly and certainly believed they would. As she relaxed, the images resolved into discrete pictures. She touched one with her consciousness and felt herself being drawn into another world.

Well, Alice, here we go down yet another rabbit hole. Let's see where this one takes me...

—⁓—

He adored his father, but then who didn't? It would be difficult not to like a man who was warm, generous and always reaching out to help everyone around him. His mom was pretty cool too, but Joey was at the age of hero worship and his dad was definitely his hero. So when they heard the woman screaming as they were walking home from baseball practice, it was no great surprise when his dad said, "Wait here and don't move." It was exciting - like in the movies where the hero gets to rescue the damsel in distress. Of course, Joey did what any eight-year-old boy would do. He ignored his father's instructions and sneaked after him. No way was he going to miss all the action!

Hiding behind some discarded boxes, Joey tried to slow his breathing as he peered around the corner. There was his super-hero dad, brandishing a big piece of pipe that he had picked up from the nearby trash heap. His father's eyes took on a steely intensity, his gaze never wavering from the three tough-looking young men standing insolently in front of him. No one paid any attention to the half-undressed girl lying on the ground curled up in a fetal position, sobbing hysterically.

"Now leave her alone and get out of here. You don't want any trouble and there's no point in us fighting. Just leave, NOW!" His dad spoke with a quiet confidence, holding the pipe as if he knew how to use it. Joey watched with horrified fascination.

"He's right. This is getting to be more trouble than it's worth. We can find easier prey somewhere else. Let's just go." The smallest of the three looked to one of the others, who was nodding in agreement.

"Not so fast," the third one sneered. "I'm the boss here. Nobody tells me what to do. You two do what I say and leave when I tell you to." He turned back to Joey's father. "If there's one thing I hate it's do-gooders trying to poke their noses where they don't belong. Face it, asshole. The world stinks and nobody really cares. So why do you waste your time trying? It's time you gave up and I'm going to help you." He pulled out a gun and coldly pulled the trigger.

Joey watched as blood gushed from his father's stomach. He heard one of the other boys shouting but for Joey, the words had turned into meaningless babble.

"What the hell did you do, Larry? You shot him. You fuckin' shot him. What do we do now?"

"We make sure the girl don't tell on us, that's what we do." He turned and this time pumped several rounds towards the girl. "Now shut up and let's get going."

Joey turned his head when he heard the shots

and saw the girl's head exploding, blood splattering everywhere. At that moment the world stopped making sense. He just stood and stared, unable to move or think. That's probably what saved his life. The young men ran off unaware that a small boy had hidden around the corner and witnessed the entire scene.

When the police found him several hours later, he had not moved a single muscle. He had watched his father bleed to death, but by that point he had retreated so far into himself that he didn't fully comprehend that his father was dead.

His mother did everything she could to reach him, and over time he improved somewhat, but remained remote. The last chance for his recovery was lost the day after his ninth birthday. His mom was chatting on the phone while cutting some vegetables. The knife slipped and she cut her finger. Joey watched as the blood dripped onto the counter. He stared at it, transfixed. Slowly his world narrowed to that one small drop of blood. His whole world turned red and he entered into that bright redness, never to return.

Chapter Seven

ALICIA REALIZED she had just experienced what some would term a "past life," yet Douglas had implied that time was interwoven and multidimensional. How then was she supposed to conceptualize what she was seeing? If she had a body, she would be shaking right now - not just because her sense of reality was thoroughly disrupted, or because the experience had been so intense. As she witnessed the scene, she had done so through the eyes of the thug who had pulled the trigger. She was trying to cope with the realization that in one of her "other incarnations" or in some other dimension, she was a brutal cold-blooded killer who had not only killed an innocent young girl, but Joey/Brian's father. In that respect, she was in some way responsible for Joey/Brian's withdrawal from life. The implications were deeply disturbing, and she had absolutely no idea what she was supposed to do about it.

This concept of the interweaving of time was mind-boggling. Did it suggest that she had just experienced a parallel world, or were these events happening simultaneously in other dimensions of the same world? She remembered Douglas's explanation but at the time, it had only made her more confused…

"Alicia, how would you describe the beauty of a sunset over the ocean to a blind man who has never seen a sunset, let alone the ocean, or for that matter has never seen a color? In many ways, we're all blind. You think the world exists in three dimensions, I believe it exists in four dimensions. Trying to describe a four-dimensional universe in three-dimensional terminology is more complex than describing the sunset to our hypothetical blind man. At least you and the blind man exist in the same universe and hold similar ideas as to its structure.

"Let's start with the following premise: Dimensions exist that you are incapable of seeing with your eyes or absorbing with your brain. Once you stop trying to make

"logical" sense of it all, you can accept that time is not linear - even though it appears to be so."

He knew that these were difficult concepts to wrestle with and could appreciate the look of utter confusion on Alicia's face. He continued. "I believe that what are referred to as mystical experiences are actually momentary glimpses of these other dimensions. Did you know that throughout time, mystics have claimed that the mind and brain can never know the Higher Realms directly? Intellect alone is incapable of fully comprehending expansive spiritual perceptions. The sages of old tell us that there are no words for what they have come to understand - it can be grasped only through experience. Yet, none of this is truly hidden from us. It is right in front of us all the time - like the cube intersecting a two-dimensional world. In essence, it is only 'hidden' by our inability to see." Douglas shook his head. "I'm trying to describe something that is beyond words and ideas. Patience, Alicia. It will make more sense as time goes on."

Time had certainly gone on, but there was only one thing Alicia understood now that she hadn't understood then. The world didn't work the way she thought it did. Not knowing what else to do, she reached her mind out to another one of the pictures hovering over Brian's head.

Chapter Eight

SHE WAS A TIMID young woman who did her job quietly and efficiently, taking pride in the ordered cleanliness of the art gallery. Each morning she swept the floor, dusted the pictures and cleaned the glass. Today was the day for cleaning the chandeliers. She set up the tall ladder in order to reach the huge one that sparkled in the center of the gallery. She nodded to the owner as he walked through the gallery, heading in her direction. Humming quietly to herself, she went about her task unaware that one of the arms of the chandelier was cracked. Noticing a small smudge, she extended her arm to reach it, instinctively grabbing the chandelier - as she always did - to maintain her balance. The cracked arm gave way. She watched with horror as it broke away and headed for the floor below her. Unfortunately, it was at that moment that the owner reached the point directly below the chandelier. The beautiful chandelier transformed into a crystal weapon. It struck the owner on the head, cracking his skull. Blood flowed onto the floor - she fainted and fell from the ladder. The owner was killed. She broke her leg in two places. The injuries sustained by this trauma caused her to limp through the rest of her life - both physically and emotionally.

This is not fun! thought Alicia as she returned once more to herself. If, as she suspected, the images currently above Brian's head had to do with violent bloody deaths leading to his withdrawing on some level, she did not relish the idea of having to experience them all. Besides, she couldn't imagine what good it was doing Brian.

OK, out there. I need some more help. Please!" Nothing happened - at least not in the way she expected it to. She started to get hunches, feelings, and stray thoughts that seemed to make sense. The strongest one went something like: "Look without looking, and see with your heart, not your eyes." She realized that so far, she had just randomly reached out to the images; now she took the time to gaze at the pictures floating above

Brian and to sense what she could about them. Not only were some more vibrant - one had a particularly strong pull. She followed it.

Chapter Nine

WHOEVER SAID "WAR IS HELL" *understated the obvious. Paul had enlisted with a sense of manly pride, ready to defeat the bad guys and make the world safe for everyone else. He didn't know that he would be the one defeated. Enemy soldiers were all around - some so close that he could hear them. Being cold, tired and hungry wasn't the worst of it; he no longer cared or even remembered why he was there. All he knew was that the enemy tried to kill him while he tried to kill the enemy. He and Gerald had been in the foxhole for what seemed like an eternity. During that eternity they had fallen into a comfortable rhythm with each other. Gerald was his lifeline, a focal point for retaining his sanity and what little remained of his humanity. When one slept, the other watched. They were all they had, now that the rest of the world had gone completely mad. "I'm sick of the blood, sick of the death, or is it that I'm sick to death - sick to death of death." He didn't feel any need to make sense and didn't expect Gerald to respond. It was just nice to hear his own voice and know that someone was alive nearby to hear him.*

It was his turn to sleep. Strange that he could now fall asleep to the sounds of gunfire and the screams of dying men. Some sixth sense roused him from sleep seconds before the enemy soldier appeared at the edge of the foxhole aiming his rifle at Gerald's back. Gerald turned and aimed his rifle, but not fast enough to pull the trigger. The soldier shot Gerald in the stomach. Paul barely had time to register how much blood was spilling from his friend's gut. Aiming his rifle, he shot round after round into the enemy soldier, screaming, "You bloody bastard! Die, you bloody bastard! ... Kill or be killed - that's what it's about... Die, bastard, die!" He ran to the bloodied body of the enemy soldier and ripped the gun out of his hand. A photo fell to the ground. He picked it up, gazed at it, and broke into uncontrollable sobs.

In the photo, the now dead soldier was smiling, his arm around a young attractive woman who looked up at him adoringly. Two young boys were standing in front of them. Next to them was an older woman beaming with pride. He held his head in his hands and continued sobbing. "I'm sorry. I'm so sorry. You aren't a bastard, you aren't even the enemy. You're a dad, a son, a husband, and I just murdered you in cold blood. I'm sorry. I'm sorry. I'm so sorry." He couldn't stop sobbing and was still crying many hours later when the action cleared enough for the medics to find him.

Though his body was not wounded, the life had been sucked out of it. He hated himself for what he had become. Now he knew what men were capable of - even the "good" ones - and so he hated everyone. Life had no purpose. Suicide might have been an option, but the thought of killing anyone - even himself - was abhorrent. So he lived, yet was not alive. Having lost his will to live, his life force weakened.

Alicia felt that she was being shown something significant. She sensed that this was the critical life she was seeking. This soul experiencing life as Paul was on the verge of deciding whether to live or die. If the young soldier chose death, it would strengthen the echo that was currently threatening Brian's life. If he chose life, Brian could gain needed insight and skills to cope with the current trauma. Paul's despair had reverberated into Brian's consciousness, the trigger having been his bloody wound and his fear that Alicia was injured through his actions as driver. The question was, what could she do to help?

The beings that had communicated with her earlier were limited in what they were allowed to do directly, yet she was beginning to suspect that they were behind her hunches and flashes of insight. The worshipper of cold hard facts was learning to respect intuition and to recognize that she was going to have to feel - not think - her way through helping Brian.

It's terrifying to realize that I don't know what's real or how the world works. What if "reality" is not a constant, but rather a fluid, mercurial state, constantly affected and altered by our thoughts and feelings, both in this and in other dimensions? Is this physical existence merely a mirror for our soul, a training ground for learning through experience? And if that's the case, what is a soul? If I had a head right now, these thoughts would be giving me a headache. But then I don't even currently have a body, do I? So who or what am I? Am I Alicia even when not in Alicia's body? These questions could make one seriously crazy. No wonder people are afraid of these ideas. She gave up trying to understand "reality."

Chapter Ten

LIKE THE OMNISCIENT narrator of a novel, Alicia was privy to feelings and thoughts that were not available to those still inhabiting and limited by their physical bodies. The experience was profound and liberating. Gaining a wealth of knowledge about the human psyche taught her that psychiatry was another area of medicine that was, from her new perspective, still an infant science. She tried to imagine Dr. Sherwood, her straight-laced, narrow minded psychiatry professor, teaching young medical students about what she was now learning…

"*Yes,*" she could hear Dr. Sherwood say, "*some of the pictures that revolve above the patient's head do pertain to the immediate childhood, but some, of course, are from other dimensions of time and space. The skill here is to learn which ones are the most relevant and then learn how to heal the patient on all dimensions."*

Well, I may have lost my body, she thought, but at least I still have my sense of humor.

She was acquiring quite an education. She now understood that the majority of people were largely "asleep" - believing that what their eyes told them was all that existed. Until recently, she had been one of them. Dr. Hardin, the doctor who had seen and spoken to her while she was out of her body in the emergency room, was more "awake" than most. People like him who functioned, or were potentially able to function, in more than just one dimension had fields of energy surrounding them that were different in ways that were hard to describe. The best words she could come up with were: more open, expansive, deeper, and more spacious.

Convinced that the key to Brian's recovery lay in his lifetime as Paul, she focused her thoughts on Paul. The result was that she found herself transported to a military psychiatric hospital where he was being held for observation. He was depressed, withdrawn, and only minimally communicative. No one seemed able to pierce his wall of despondency. Could she? In her hospital room, Dr. Hardin had sensed her presence and communicated with her, but was this possible in reverse? Paul was not one of the "awake" ones and she could see no way to reach or affect him. She had to find a way. Selfishly, she wanted to succeed in order to save Brian, but now she realized that many other "lives" were also at stake.

What's the use of all this knowledge if I'm not able to use it? I understand Paul better than he understands himself, and certainly better than his doctors and nurses. I can "see" what would help him, but I can't do anything from out here! Is his soul destined to be trapped in an endless cycle of trauma, leading to withdrawal? Why am I being shown all this if I can't make a difference? I need help! And..." she started mumbling softly *"and frankly, I'm disappointed that the capacity for frustration can survive outside the physical body. Is this fair? I lose my body but get to keep my neuroses...*

Chapter Eleven

ALICIA CONTINUED studying Paul's life, looking for a way to help. An idea began to form when she broadened her search to include everyone Paul came into contact with. Julia, one of his nurses, had an unusually open energy field and was highly sensitive to vibrations from levels beyond her immediate physical surroundings. She tried communicating with her directly but was unsuccessful. Though uncertain as to how to proceed, Alicia felt encouraged to enlist this young woman's aid. Following this hunch, she stopped focusing on Paul and turned her attention to Julia. "Come on, Julia. There must be a reason I'm being drawn to you. Show me what it is."

Through trial and error, Alicia was learning the social graces of being a disembodied spirit. The rules of etiquette were not that different from those of the physical plane of existence. Her interest in Julia didn't give her the right to pry into her life or try to influence her. She had to ask permission and be invited in. She hadn't understood this earlier. Brian had tacitly given his permission and wanted her help. With Julia the process was more formal. When she first tried to communicate and connect with Julia, she was met by what felt like an impenetrable barrier, and when she had tried to study Julia's life, she encountered what felt like a wall of disapproval.

"What's the matter, Julia? Don't you want me here?" As soon as she asked the question she felt the wall of disapproval soften. "Is that it? Am I intruding without permission? I just want to help Paul. Are you willing to try to help me?"

She was surprised to hear a response. "I thank you for letting your needs and wishes be known. I have felt your presence, but it is not proper for you to attempt interaction before permission is granted. I also felt the goodness of your intent, so did not send you away. In the cycle where this soul is known as Julia, the need to be of service is strong. Julia must have free will to decide how to respond, but permission is granted for you to try and enlist her aid. Julia, in your terminology, is not "awake enough" to be aware of this communication and there is now no need for us to communicate further. I wish you blessings and success. Your goal is a worthy one."

"Thank you. Please understand that no disrespect was meant. I'm new to all this and this is the first time I've tried to focus on someone other than the person known - in this cycle - as Paul. I'm trying to figure out why I'm drawn to Julia and how she can help me with Paul." Having defined her wishes, Alicia found herself transported to a coffee shop where a conversation was taking place between Julia and a friend. Before floating closer, she silently requested permission to observe, and felt permission being granted.

"Come on, Sara. You don't really believe in that stuff, do you? When I was a kid, there was a woman in my town who claimed to be a medium who could talk to all your 'dearly departed' loved ones. She was a fraud and finally got caught. Most of them are charlatans, you know."

"I know, Julia, but this lady is for real. Honestly. You just have to meet her! And she isn't a medium. She calls herself a 'sensitive.' She says she picks up messages from beings on other planes. Come on, Julia. Come with me. Please, just this once..."

"You've got to be kidding. Sara, she's probably trying to swindle money from you. You're so sweet - and way too gullible. You really shouldn't go to those things. Look, this war has affected all of us and I know it's tempting to believe that there's more to the world than the horrors we've all been through, but seriously, Sara, don't go flying off into some fantasy world. Deal with reality. Otherwise, you might become like some of those soldiers we work with who have withdrawn from life. 'Other planes?' Really Sara, that's stretching things a bit too far."

Alicia chuckled to herself. *I remember a time when I didn't believe in those 'other planes' either, but that was before I found myself on one. Yes, come on, Julia. This might be just the opening I've been waiting for. Aren't you even curious? Please, Julia. I need your help and I don't know how to reach you.* She projected to Julia an image of Sara's naive innocence in need of protection. Then she added her own personal plea. *Not only can you help and support your friend; you may be able to help me and help Paul as well.* She focused on sending Julia positive images of the spiritual meeting.

Julia shook her head. "I don't know, Sara. I don't believe in any of this kind of stuff, but I guess I'll go just to keep an eye on you. It's strange, but I just have a sense that I should go."

Chapter Twelve

THE AUDITORIUM was cozy and bright. On the stage were two chairs facing forward. Margaret walked to the front of the room and proceeded to sit in the chair that - like herself - was well padded. She smiled calmly, her round, full face radiating serenity. A moment later a woman who looked like a younger version of Margaret took the chair next to her and turned it so that she could face her mother rather than the audience.

Julia instinctively liked the woman, perhaps because she looked so grandmotherly that one almost expected her to start passing out milk and cookies. *Keep your guard up, Julia reminded herself. Good con people always look perfectly harmless and charming.*

"Good evening." Margaret's voice was gentle and

soothing. "I see several new faces tonight so I will begin with an explanation of what you will experience here. First, this is not a séance. As you can see, the room is well lit. You don't have to hold hands with your neighbor and you will be able to see me clearly at all times. There will be no ectoplasmic manifestations, or displays of strange feats by spirits of the departed. I am a messenger for those beings of a higher vibrational level that reside in the Great Beyond. They will use my physical vehicle - my body - as a means to communicate their wisdom to you. I will be unaware of much of what goes on during this time, so my daughter will be here if any assistance is needed. I need a moment to prepare. We will begin shortly."

Alicia was uncomfortably aware that her plane of existence was getting increasingly crowded. Like bees drawn to a flower, disembodied spirits were being drawn to Margaret's vibration - and she could tell that not all were what Margaret had called 'beings of a higher vibrational level."

Margaret closed her eyes and focused her heart on her desire to be of service. She began softly intoning a prayer, calling upon God and the angels to protect and guide her as she opened herself to helping and healing those around her that evening. Alicia watched with fascination as Margaret's energy field shifted. As it changed, many of the lower-vibrational spirits left. She felt herself being gently pushed away, but not to the point of having to leave.

"No. Wait!" Alicia had no idea who she might be speaking to. "I'm not here for myself, but to help a loved one. There is one at this meeting who can help him, and I wish to give her a message." She felt an alien presence touch her consciousness. Sensing its wisdom and depth, she felt no fear. It was humbling to once again realize how little she knew or understood about existence. "Who or what are you? Are you an aspect of Margaret's soul?" she asked.

"It matters not what I am. If you need a label, think of me as the gatekeeper. I determine who is fit to pass through. You are still connected to a physical form, and on this plane you are as yet uncultivated. However, you radiate goodness from your heart and your purpose here is pure. To bring you through will demand much from both you and the host, but all of your paths are interconnected. It is proper for this to take place. It will be difficult, but can restore much harmony. Come forward. You will be the first."

Alicia didn't have much time to wonder what it meant to be first. The sensation was like being gently sucked into a cyclone. Immediately everything felt different. For the second time since her world had been turned upside down, she was deeply afraid. She felt trapped as a sense of great pressure descended upon her. She had to remind herself that she couldn't be suffocating because she had no body and therefore no lungs that needed air. That thought triggered the realization of what had taken place. She was back in a body - it just wasn't her own body. Everything felt wrong and once again she felt panic rising.

"Relax, child. You're not trapped here. If you want to use this vehicle to communicate, you must settle down. Focus on what you want to accomplish. I can't surrender control when you're so agitated. Either you learn to calm yourself or I will have to send you on your way. This is most distressing for me, and my physical form can't handle this stress for long. Stop fighting me. I can help you but we must work together. It will feel very different from what you are used to because you are not fully connected to this form, but use it as you would your own body. Slowly now. See? You're getting it. OK. I'm going to recede into the background now. This may be the only chance you'll have - so say whatever you need to say."

The panic faded and Alicia glanced around the room through Margaret's eyes. She saw that Margaret's daughter was looking at her with concern. She directed her first attempt to speak to her.

"It's OK. It just took me a moment to figure it all out. No need for concern." The daughter nodded her understanding and Alicia switched her focus to the sea of faces in front of her. Many in the audience were lost and hungry for direction, willing to grasp at any straw they could find. The realization was daunting. She was aware that she could say anything she wanted and that they would take it as a message from a "Higher Being from the Great Beyond." This was not as it should be, and she felt compelled to do something about it.

"Greetings. I think it is important for all of you here tonight to know that there are many beings on different planes of existence that are capable of communicating, as I am. Not all of them are Enlightened Souls or particularly Higher Beings. It's good to keep an open mind, but also a skeptical one. Beings not currently in a physical body are not necessarily wiser than any of you sitting in this room. They can see more; this doesn't mean they know more." She felt she had the authority to say this as a person who just a short time ago had been in a physical body herself. She may have learned some interesting things, but she certainly didn't feel any wiser just because she had been ejected from her body. "The one whose body I currently communicate through is sincere and is doing all she can to ensure the quality of what comes through her, but it is still wise to test information received in this form.

"I have a message for one of you sitting here this evening." She looked directly at Julia. "I know you have a healthy skepticism about this and I respect that. I also understand that dropping that skepticism and believing in what you see here tonight will completely alter your sense of reality and most likely change the direction of your life. I don't want to stir up a crisis for you, and I'm not even sure if I have the right to ask this of you, but I need your help. Julia, you have a big heart and I know you care about the soldiers you work with. You're a wonderful and dedicated nurse." She watched Julia pale and remembered how her first short conversation with Douglas had stirred ripples of change in her life. She hoped that Julia's changes, like her own, would be positive ones. "I don't have very much time here, so I will have to be very direct. You work with a young soldier named Paul who has withdrawn from much of life. Are you willing to work with me to help him?"

"Who told you all this? How could you know?"

Alicia in Margaret's body sighed. She was beginning to understand how Douglas affected people so deeply and so quickly. She looked with her Inner Eye at Julia, focusing on a picture above her head that strongly called to her.

"I know about it the same way I know about your rag doll Susie. I know how you talked to her and how she helped you deal with your mom's death. It was only by telling Susie all your secrets that you overcame that devastating and lonely time in your life. It's why you're so drawn to encouraging the soldiers to talk to you. You know the power of sharing and you try to be their Susie. It's a beautiful and noble act. You've helped more people than you realize. I also know you've never shared this with anyone. Please don't be frightened that I know this. I say this only to show you that I know things. I also know things about the soldier you call Paul. Would you help me help him heal?"

Alicia could see that Julia was deeply shaken, but she also sensed a part of her soul awakening as she absorbed what she was hearing. Yes, she was beginning to understand more about Douglas's effect on people.

"What is it you want me to do?" Julia asked in a tentative voice.

Alicia took a moment to collect her thoughts. Many in the audience thought of her as some wise mystical teacher. They would hang on her every word. She wondered what they would think if she explained to them that she had been no different from them until an accident had thrown her out of her body. She directed her gaze at Julia.

"Everyone around Paul is trying to get him to deal with the trauma. Paul doesn't need to deal with the trauma; he needs to deal with the solution. Devastated both by the destruction he has caused as well as by what he has seen wrought by others, he needs to immerse himself in rebuilding and healing. In another of his soul's incarnations, he is a doctor devoted to saving life, not destroying it. But in this cycle he has given up. I know that some of the nurses at the hospital have been talking about starting an organization to help families who have lost loved ones in the war. He has the abilities needed to help start and run this organization. Stop treating him as an invalid and enlist his aid. He is racked with guilt and needs to feel that he is helping others - particularly families."

Julia now looked at her reverently. "I will do as you say. Thank you."

"Julia, do only what your heart tells you is right. Don't give me your power by doing this for me. I'm no wiser than you - I just see more." Alicia smiled as she caught a glimpse of Julia's future. The organization would become very successful under Paul and Julia's direction. But that was not what had made her smile. It was the glimpse of them beaming at each other on their wedding day. Her work here was done. It was time to check on Brian and hopefully to finally return to her own body.

Chapter Thirteen

DR. HARDIN WAS THERE with the young intern when Alicia returned to her spot in the upper right corner of her hospital room. Glancing up at her, he nodded and told the young intern that the patient would be waking up shortly. He then sent the intern on a task, thereby leaving him alone in her room.

"The young man will be fine. He's still working out some things but will probably awaken later today. Time feels different where you are - you've only been gone for about an hour of our time. Don't worry. Neither of you have been comatose for long. He reached out to her still form, placing his hand on hers, and she felt herself being pulled back to her body. She realized that he was helping her come back.

She was glad to return, but saddened by losing the feeling of spacious freedom she had become accustomed to. After her experience in Margaret's body, she was better prepared for being "squished" back into physical form. She moved her arms and legs, testing the feel of it, and slowly opened her eyes.

"Welcome back, Alicia. Can you hear me?" Dr. Hardin looked at her kindly. "You're OK, and so is your friend Brian. You had an auto accident and hit your head. You've been unconscious for a little over an hour, but you're fine."

Alicia felt confused. Had it all been a dream? Why was Dr. Hardin acting as if he had no knowledge of what had taken place? The images were starting to get a bit hazy. She took a moment to gather her memories. Dream or not, she didn't want to lose them. She probably would have refrained from saying anything had she been more alert, but she was still a bit disoriented.

"Don't you remember? You talked right to me and instructed me on how to proceed. The source of the problem was rooted in Brian's experiences as Paul. Did you know that in another dimension you're called Margaret, and as Margaret you help heal others by letting spirits give messages to people by talking through you? So you ended up helping me there as well as here. But, now you're acting as if none of it is real. It wasn't just a dream. I'm sure of it."

Dr. Hardin looked at her with a merry twinkle in his eyes. "How absolutely delightful. In all my seventy-three years, you're the first one who actually remembered. There was only one other who understood what was happening, and that one changed my life forever. Sadly, most forget as soon as they awaken. Tell me everything. We have time before anyone else comes into the room."

When she finished she looked at Dr. Hardin. "So, now that I've told you my story, I want to hear yours. How did it come about that you see and communicate with people's consciousness outside of their bodies? Your turn now."

"Well, that seems fair. Here goes. We still have a bit more time, so I'll share my story with you.

Chapter Fourteen

DR HARDIN SMILED at Alica as he began his story. "My grandpa always told me to be a good boy and do everything my mom and dad said or else the boogeyman would come and get me. That's what set the stage for my interpretation of what happened. The first time was when I was around six years old. I woke up in the middle of the night and saw an old man sitting at the foot of my bed. The man looked distraught as he wailed, "I've been a selfish geezer and now it's too late! Where am I? I have to get back!" I just started screaming and what I assumed was the boogeyman disappeared."

"I tried to tell my parents about it, but they just said it was a bad dream and I should forget about it. My brother teased me and threatened me with the boogeyman's return if I wasn't good. But I knew it wasn't a dream and I couldn't forget about it. After a while, the fear faded, and that might have been the end of it - except that a year later something similar happened. After that, I kept seeing people who, according to everyone else, weren't there. I stopped talking about these visions after I overheard a conversation between my mom and dad.

"Remember at that point I was eight years old, so you can imagine my reaction to hearing my dad say he was concerned that I wasn't right in the head and that maybe they should take me to what he called a 'head-shrinker.' Not knowing what that was made it sound terrifying; but my mom's reaction was even more frightening. She said there was no way she was going to risk having a son of hers locked up in some kind of loony bin with a bunch of crazy people. It was bad enough that her brother Mickey was crazy; she wasn't going to go through that again with her son. I knew that no one in the family wanted to talk to - let alone talk about - my uncle Mickey, and I didn't want the same fate. So when I heard her say she was sure it was just a phase and that I would grow out of it, I took that as my cue. I resolved that I would never again mention these folks that no one else could see - and I stuck by that resolve. Unfortunately, not talking about them didn't make them go away. I didn't know what they were and I didn't know what to do about them. I assumed that I was crazy and had to hide that fact from everyone around me. I became a loner, but figured that was better than getting thrown into an asylum. By the time I turned sixteen, I was a tad strange, but at least no one accused me of being crazy or threatened to lock me up.

"The year of my sixteenth birthday, my mom's brother Mickey came for a visit. I really liked him, but everyone seemed determined to keep me from spending too much time with him because of his being crazy.

"Seems he came home because he knew he was dying. There wasn't much time left and he wanted to heal things with his family while he still could. There was a bunch of crying and hugging and next thing I knew Mickey was going to live with us until he died. He went downhill pretty fast from there, and soon he was bedridden. We knew he was close to death.

"One day as I was sitting in the living room reading a book, I sensed a 'presence' around me. At that point, that's what I called it when I could see someone no one else could. It was hard to ignore the feeling so I looked up and got one heck of a shock. This presence was like none that I had ever seen before - I recognized this one. It was my uncle Mickey. I opened my mouth to speak to him, but immediately he put his finger to his lips, indicating that I should remain silent. I stared transfixed and watched him slowly fade and disappear. A few minutes later my mom came out of Mickey's room. I figured that he had died and that I had just seen his spirit. I was starting to see my life and my 'craziness' in a whole new light.

"My mom told me that my uncle Mickey was real close to death and for a moment they had believed he was gone. He was still alive, though just barely, and he wanted to speak to me - alone. I went into his room and, a minute later, walked out of that room a different person. I'll never forget that conversation." Sam Hardin got a faraway look in his eyes as he recalled the conversation…

"I'm sorry, Sammy. I didn't know you could see them too. They told me I was crazy and wanted to lock me up, so I had to leave. Never occurred to me that anyone else in the family had the same ability. Listen kid, not much time. Quite an effort for me to come back but I had to let you know. Some are people who just died. I'm sure you'll see me again when I leave my body the final time. That's not all they are. A lot of them have this silver cord attached to them. Those ones aren't dead. Some of them are just asleep and trying to figure stuff out in their dreams. Others are unconscious and in comas - those are usually pretty lost and need help. You have the ability to help them - I know it. You're not crazy but people will think you are if you talk about it. Wish I could say more but this is all I can do. Good luck, kid. Gotta close my eyes now..."

Sam pulled himself back to the present and looked at Alicia. "So, once I started to understand it all, I set my sights on becoming a doctor specializing in working with comatose head traumas - and here I am. Look, Alicia. I have to warn you. You'll find that you can't talk about this - not even to those you're closest too. People can't understand until they've experienced if for themselves. Believing in it, really believing, starts to awaken a different kind of awareness and a shift in perception. This stuff threatens people's sense of reality, and people don't like having their worldviews messed with. When that starts to happen, most people accuse anybody who believes in this stuff of being crazy. You'll get used to it, but at times it will make you feel pretty alone. Keep in touch and call me anytime you need someone to talk to. Well, take it easy and rest up. I'm going to go check on your friend Brian."

Chapter Fifteen

ALICIA'S EXPERIENCES changed her. At first she expected all the changes to be positive - after all, she had gained a much broader view of life, in which everything and everyone was interconnected in a sacred dance. Yet, the next few months were not easy. The difficulties occurred in two separate but related areas. Both involved a sense of isolation and loneliness.

Having experienced the freedom of being beyond her physical form, she now realized how isolated and cut off souls were when in human bodies. She had tasted what it was like to be entwined with everything around her, and the loss was devastating. At times, she was so consumed with trying to get back to that state that nothing else would satisfy her. Over time, and with the help of many long conversations with Sam Hardin, she adjusted, but the hunger and longing remained strong.

Once she readjusted to the limitations of an embodied soul, she was ready to absorb the profound lessons she had been shown. However, she learned that she did indeed have to keep much of what she had experienced to herself. When she tried to share it, some people thought it was a fascinating product of an overactive imagination. Others believed she was the possessor of "otherworldly" powers and wanted her to guide them and answer all their questions. Still others thought she was crazy and using these ideas to avoid life's "real" challenges. Not that long ago, she would have been one of those accusing her of using fantasy to avoid reality. As Sam Hardin had warned her, people who had not had the experiences themselves could not understand. It was particularly difficult to be around those who were threatened by what she had seen. They were the ones who attacked her sanity. Once again, it was Sam who helped her through. It was a relief to have at least one person she could talk to. While grateful, this also emphasized the most painful part of what she was going through: she couldn't talk to Brian about any of it. The first time she tried, he looked concerned and asked about her head injury, wondering if perhaps she was having residual effects. The second time, before she could say very much, he made a joke about how vivid her "dreams" had been while unconscious. The third time, he just changed the subject. She loved Brian, but realized that if they were to stay together, there were some things they wouldn't be able to share. Yet, as a result of what she had been through, she was happier and more at peace. She accepted and finally resigned herself to being unable to communicate much of what she had learned. Life settled into a pleasant routine, and six months later she and Brian became engaged to be married.

Chapter Sixteen

ALICIA WAS ON DUTY when Douglas Fairway was once again admitted to the hospital. No one had heard from him in over a year. Though sorry that he was back in the hospital, this time Alicia was excited at the prospect of seeing him. As soon as she entered his room, she could tell that his condition was not good.

"Well, look who's here." He studied her for a moment. "Ah, I see. Very good. I can die a happy man; my work here is done." He flashed his wonderful smile, but Alicia could see that smiling was an effort.

Alicia ran to him and threw her arms around him. "Douglas, I can't tell you how glad I am to see you. I have so much to share with you. But first, who is in charge of your case? Let me see your chart. I'll see what we can do for you. No offense, but you look terrible." She tried to smile as she spoke, but suddenly felt tears forming.

"Dear Alicia, tears are a wonderful thing, but don't waste yours on me. I'm delighted that your heart has opened and healed. Your life is just beginning; mine has reached its end. Ah, but what a wonderful journey this one has been! Dear child, you understand now. Death is not something to fear. I will continue on and we shall continue to interact. Just not as Douglas and Alicia. We have helped each other countless times, and continue to do so. I am at peace. Besides, I have grown weary of this body. In this life, my wife and children were killed in an accident, and I have learned much about loneliness. I have lived many years without my family, and I miss them terribly. There is nothing more I need to do as Douglas. I'm ready to leave. Yes, you will miss me, but know that I'm not abandoning you. I'm just finished with this particular incarnation. There are so many others, so many..." He paused and closed his eyes. "Dear girl, I can't talk much longer. I believe I need to rest."

"Douglas, may I ask you a question?"

"Certainly, child. What is it?"

"You said once that you came here because of me.

What did you mean?"

Douglas opened his eyes and smiled his special smile. "I did indeed. And you will have your answer. Just not in this cycle of time. Know that I love you, Alicia, and we shall always be connected. Don't grieve too much." One last time she heard his quicksilver laugh. "Death and I are old and dear friends. You're beginning to understand that now. Enjoy your life. The glimpses that I see of it tell me that this one will be quite a good one. Go now. I must sleep." And with that, he closed his eyes and drifted off into a peaceful sleep.

When the time came for Douglas to leave his body, his spirit visited Alicia one last time. He gazed at her lovingly and sent her his blessings. His soul was filled with joy to see that Alicia was indeed content. He knew that this time around she would enjoy a long and happy life.

BOOK TWO

B O O K   T W O

Chapter One

*TUMBLING THROUGH space... Watching...
Observing...Breaking into thousands of small pieces,
each orbiting in different directions... Each segment
screamed in pain, longing for a return to wholeness.
Myriad images... countless stories... He and his mother
were being dragged through the jungle and he was
afraid... She was old as she exhaled her last breath...
The rage was so powerful it threatened to tear him apart
and made him want to hurt others as he had been hurt...
She was blessed to know the peace and the security of
a deep love... Her emotions were dangerous and could
overwhelm her if she didn't close them off. A sterile life
would be safer than a painful one...With dizzying speed
she whirled from one experience to the other.*

"We are all one," a voice that was her - but not her - insisted. It spoke with a tension that bespoke fear, continually stressing the importance of her understanding and remembering. "Of course," thought Nadjia. "How could I forget what even the smallest of children understand - that everything is interconnected and that all is One." "Don't forget! Don't forget! Don't Forget!" the voice repeated over and over again. She understood. Everything would be fine - as long as she could remember... Remember what? The message was important, but she could not quite grasp it...

Nadjia awoke. Tension radiated from her usually serene countenance as she recalled her Dream Time. Many of the worlds she had traversed were incomprehensible, and much of what the voice had said made little sense, yet with every fiber of her body she still felt the urgency with which it wanted her to remember. Later, she would bring her dream to the Dream Woman to find out more of its meaning, but for now she pushed it aside, unwilling to allow anything to mar the sweet delight and anticipation that filled her. The Tetwonee people had great respect for their ceremonies, their Holy Men, and the Spirits that helped guide their lives; and today, Nadjia would experience the most sacred ceremony of their village. Eighteen times had the seasons come and gone since her birth, and today was the day that Gandje, the village Holy Man, would conduct her Honoring Ceremony. Today, at last, the Spirits would indicate her rightful place in the community.

Her hands shook as she smoothed out the ceremonial robe she would be wearing. Before she donned the robe, she would brush her unruly locks until they agreed to behave, for she wanted to look beautiful. She knew she should be focusing on her preparations, but right now her shining eyes and wide grin had little to do with the impending ceremony. It was so like Nardjol to choose the day before her ceremony to present her with the Quala necklace he had made for her. Her eyes took on a faraway, dreamy look…

—∿∿—

She had always known that she and Nardjol would wed, so when he presented her with the Quala, she began to reach for it eagerly. Catching herself in time, she demurely folded her hands in her lap, reminding herself of the importance of waiting until the Spirits could communicate with her in the Dream Time. She kept her voice calm as she intoned the ancient ritual response: "You honor me by your offer. Tonight I sleep with your Quala to see what the Spirits will say. If they send warnings, I will not accept. If they send blessings, I will wear the Quala tomorrow so that all may know we are promised to each other as Mates of the Soul for the entirety of this cycle we share upon this earth."

She remembered with crystal clarity all that had taken place that night in the Dream Time and the following morning with Kora the Dream Woman…

Filled with excitement, she had feared she would have difficulty falling asleep. But, the Night Wisps soothed her and breathed her into the dream state…

In the first dream, she had huddled in an unfamiliar space, alone and abandoned. Even the light had forsaken her. The darkness frightened her until she heard the voice. "Greetings, Child." The resonant tones embraced her and were a balm to her fear. "Many are the paths you will wander, many are the trials you will encounter - all are but fires of initiation to take you to your final destiny. You are not alone. I shall be with you whenever you have need of me." The voice - so tantalizingly familiar - assured her that out of the depth of darkness would come the greatest illumination. Reassured, she relaxed into a deeper sleep and entered her second dream...

In front of her stood Nardjol, but not as she usually saw him. A translucent golden light surrounded him, emanating from the purity of his soul. Reaching for him, she felt herself falling through an opening in his heart. Now floating in beautifully colored currents of light, she was filled with wonder as she realized that they were formed from the depth of his love for her. The voice returned and whispered, "Don't forget. No matter how great one's Faith, even the smallest doubt may erode it..."

In the third and final dream, Nadjia saw her spirit glowing with fiercely bright intensity. She watched as it rose above her body. In the distance she saw Nardjol's spirit also rise from his body. They floated toward each other, and then in different directions, always maintaining a strong fiery link between them. The link spanned eons, but she was unable to see the stories that over time they had woven together. Their spirits rejoiced in their connection until a fog suddenly obscured her vision. She shrank

from it in fear. "Remember, you are not alone," said the
voice. Turning back, she faced her fear and her faith grew
stronger. She calmly knew that the fog would lift and all
would be as it was meant to be. She wandered through the
fog, no longer afraid...

The following morning, as the first rays of Sun
touched the earth, Nadjia awakened and began the
sacred rite of Dream Retrieval. She brought the dreams to
Kora, the Dream Woman, and waited impatiently while
Kora interpreted the messages the Spirits had sent. The
dream communications were seen as a blessing on their
union. As the Sun lifted higher into the sky, Nadjia left
Kora's dwelling, her heart singing, and Nardjol's Quala
around her neck.

—⚉—

Softly touching the Quala, Nadjia whispered, "Oh, Mother.
I wish you could be here to share this time with me! Then
my happiness would be complete." Nadjia wondered, as
she often did, what life would have been like if the Gods
had not taken her mother and father from her, leaving her
to the unfortunate necessity of being raised by Damaya,
her mother's sister.

Once again her mind drifted away from her preparations for the Honoring Ceremony, this time to unpleasant memories from her past…

—⚏—

"By the Gods, Nadjia! Can't you do anything right? What am I to do with you?" While Aunt Damaya paused for breath, Nadjia took the opportunity to listen to the symphony of sound all around her, knowing it would be but a small interlude before her aunt resumed her tirade. Imagining herself at a Ceremony of Thanks, she pretended that each sound represented a different musical instrument playing sacred songs. The bird's sweet, soothing song accompanied the agitated bark of the distant coyote, both blending with her aunt's loud sigh, which became a counterpoint to the creaking of the stool that bore her aunt's rather impressive girth. She imagined the wooden stool singing its own sad song lamenting the strain it was experiencing, creaking and groaning with every movement her aunt made.

"If your mother had not spoiled you, perhaps… Well, I do this for your dear mother whose spirit is with the Gods. I suppose it's an opportunity for me to learn patience." The next big sigh indicated that this was a lesson she had not

learned particularly well.

"Your lies are as big and as gross as everything else about you - the only things bigger are your greed and your selfishness." Nadjia longed to say these thoughts aloud, but had learned long ago that the consequences would not be worth the small satisfaction of speaking her mind. In the safe privacy of her mind, she thought, "Aunt Damaya, why can't you see past your need for being favored? The recognition and respect given to my mother came from who she was, not from the Orb. She never tried to hurt you. She loved you - though I can't see why, since you were always so cruel to her." Tears threatened as she thought of her mother, leaving her only vaguely aware that her aunt was rattling on, listing Nadjia's shortcomings and failures. She had heard it all so many times before...

Nadjia shook the memory from her mind. "What made you so bitter a soul, Damaya?" she thought. "I could have loved you if you had let me - if you had been less cruel."

—⟋⟍—

Donning the ceremonial robe, she left her dwelling to meet with Gandje. Nadjia walked slowly, head down, deep in somber thoughts about the significance of this most special of days.

Hearing a group of laughing children running through the village lightened her mood as she imagined a child of her own running with them. Raising her head, she noticed her beloved Nardjol standing strong and proud beside Kora, the Dream Woman, and her heart swelled with joy. His muscular, compact body spoke of physical prowess and power -a man not to be taken lightly. As he caught her eye, his face lit up - as it did every time he saw her - rewarding her with a glimpse of his crooked smile. Not all would say his dark, craggy face was handsome, but to her it was perfect. Certainly the Gods could not have made her a more ideal mate. Their eyes met and Nardjol gazed fondly at his beloved. Nadjia's radiant happiness and joyous excitement emphasized the fact that she had grown into a stunningly beautiful woman. Her brown eyes radiated depth and intelligence, and her lustrous dark hair hung in thick unruly waves reaching nearly to her waist, lending her an air of a wild creature of the forest. Each movement of her tall, lithe body was a study in grace and sensuality. Her beauty was not just her features or figure, though both were certainly pleasing; it came from something deep within - something unique and special.

Gandje, the village Holy Man, sensing this special something, had kept a sharp eye on Nadjia, daughter of Olaya, observing and influencing her life without her knowledge. Today was the day of her Honoring Ceremony, a day of celebration. No one noticed the heavy aura of concern Gandje carried on this day meant for joy.

Chapter Two

THEY MET in an open pavilion in the center of the village. Damaya sat, expecting Gandje to sit across from her, but Gandje remained standing, peering down at her sternly. "Before I instruct you, I must tell you that I am disappointed in you, Damaya, for you have not treated Nadjia like a daughter. Still, you are her closest family and will therefore stand in for her mother during the ceremony - though in truth you have not properly earned this right. But, it is as it is. Listen, for I have much to tell you." Damaya lowered her eyes while Gandje instructed her, unable to meet his cold and penetrating gaze. When at last he was finished, Damaya rose to bow her respect but still could not directly meet his eyes.

"Thank you, Gandje. I understand what it is you

wish me to do." She hoped the respectful tone she forced into her voice would mask the tension that bristled throughout her body. She turned and began walking briskly away, wanting time to be alone, and bumped straight into Nadjia, who was on her way to her own meeting with Gandje.

"Oh, it's you," Damaya said contemptuously. Feeling Gandje's eyes still upon her, she took a deep breath and forced her lips into what could roughly be taken as a smile. Carefully, she softened her voice. "Why, you look beautiful today, my dear. I am so very happy for you. It will be an honor to be a part of your ceremony." Nadjia responded to Damaya's seeming gentleness with gratitude, too full of excitement to notice the darkness that haunted Damaya's eyes.

Chapter Three

THE CEREMONY was soon to begin, and Nadjia stood off to the side, quietly awaiting her cue to come forward. Villagers gathered around the sacred meeting circle. Gandje sat in the center, surrounded by four blazing torches. In front of him was a beautifully woven multi-hued mat with designs that only he understood. This was the mat on which Nadjia would sit during the ceremony.

As Gandje stood up, sunlight reflecting off his Ceremonial Robe, he radiated both peace and power. The deep wrinkles etched into his skin spoke of wisdom that had come with living many seasons, yet he carried himself straight and tall. Despite his advanced age, his eyes were vibrant and youthful, and his small body was strong beyond what its appearance suggested. As he began to speak, he lifted his thin arms into the air. "Before this day, Nadjia lived with her family and was dutiful to that family. After this day, she lives with the village, and first and foremost will be dutiful to the village. Today she takes her rightful place as determined by the Gods. Today she is no longer a child. Damaya, long have you cared for her and prepared her for this day. Do you relinquish her now to the Gods and to the village?"

"Yes, it is time. Long has she been as daughter to me. Now she will be daughter to the village. Let the Gods determine her place. I set her free." Damaya woodenly intoned the ceremonial words.

The villagers listened eagerly to hear what Gandje would say next, for this part of the ceremony was never the same.

"And what legacy do you give her as you set her free?"

"I give her a legacy from her mother. I give her the gift of the Orb of Knowing, the Orb that was once her mother's. I give this first to you, Gandje, so that you may transfer its power to her." Tension radiated from Damaya's body as she repeated the phrases Gandje had instructed her to say.

Nadjia paled as she heard these words, barely aware of the stunned intake of breath from many of the villagers. The Orb had sat dormant since her mother's death. She had laid eyes on it only once, but would never forget its magnificent radiance. It was a small, multifaceted gemstone that was beautiful beyond words and imbued with sacred powers that could only be imparted to one chosen by the Gods. The chosen one would go through a ceremony and in time would be able to see that which others could not see, and to heal in ways that others could not heal.

"So be it." intoned Gandje. He paused, allowing the impact of his words to register. His voice softened as he continued. "When the sickness crept through our village and took as its prey the mother and father of Nadjia, it was a great blow to our people. For Nadjia's father was to be my student and successor, and Nadjia's mother was strong in the Gift of Knowing That Which Can Not Be Seen, as well as in the Gift of Healing. I could not understand why the Gods saw fit to take away two such strong and bright spirits. But we accept their wisdom, even when we cannot understand it. Perhaps the Gods have left us a gift in their stead by giving us their

daughter, but I do not know the whims of the Gods."
Gandje's voice had taken on a somber, almost sad tone.
"I only know that today we honor Nadjia, who embodies
the strength of spirit carried by both her mother and
her father. Last night the Dream Gods instructed me to
perform the ceremony that transfers the power from the
Orb of Knowing before the Sun completes its present
journey through the sky. The Spirits now wish to speak,
and I do their bidding. Come, Nadjia, it is time."

Nadjia stepped forward and sat upon the multi-
hued mat. She looked at the four burning torches and at
Gandje, who was sitting across from her with closed eyes.
He began the silent rituals for calling forth the spirits so
that they could speak through him. Suddenly, all four
torches dimmed as if an unseen wind had inhaled their
power. At the same moment, Gandje's eyes opened. Like
the flames of the torches, his eyes began to alter. Now
both eyes and torches took on a blazing intensity.

"Greetings, Daughter of Sorrow." The voice came
from Gandje's mouth but did not sound like his or
anyone else's voice, but more like a blending of many
sounds that were not quite voices coming from an
unearthly source. "Yes, that is what we name you -

Daughter of Sorrow." An eerie sound that could have been a sigh escaped from Gandje's lips. "From our vantage point, this fork on the path is brief, and the time of trial but a fleeting moment. For all that is yet to transpire has already been resolved. You are already whole - if only you could know so and therefore be so now, as well as then. You are a Daughter of Spirit. A Child of Spirit is uncommon, and their life paths tend to be unique and frequently challenging. You hunger for Union of Body and Spirit, and for Union of Heaven and Earth above all else. You chose this path when you were still among us. It may not seem like an easy one from your limited perspective, but we see the beauty of its wholeness. Know this: You are never truly alone.

"Ah, Child. If only you could understand what our words truly mean: you are a Healer of the Human Family, and the first one you will fully heal will be yourself. This is your Path, this is your test, this is your chosen way of achieving Wholeness. We send you blessings, Child. We send you blessings of love and strength and tenderness. We send you the blessing of Faith. These are the only tools you will need. Remember that these gifts are within you and therefore cannot be lost or taken away. Remember this even if you forget all else. We can say no more at this time. A true Child of Spirit makes its own destiny. We cannot tell you your place within this or any other community. It is for you to determine. If we could shoulder your pain for you, we would do so. But to do so would cripple you and make you unfit for the glorious destiny that is yours. Know that you are loved. Blessings, Child. We have no more to say at this time. We leave you now."

The torches dimmed once again. Gandje's body remained totally still. Slowly the torches returned to their normal brightness, and as they did so, Gandje opened his eyes. Nadjia was surprised to see those eyes were filled with tears. He looked at her solemnly, then turned and faced the villagers.

"The Spirits have spoken. The Honoring Ceremony is done. Before the Sun has completed this day's journey, Nadjia will come to me and I will perform the Ceremony of Transference of Power from the Orb to her. In the fullness of time and when the Power has ripened within her soul, then shall she have the Knowledge of That Which Can't Be Seen, and then shall she have the Power of a Healer. We are not to know when this time will be, nor are we to know how she will serve the village with these powers. As a Child of Spirit it is for her to discover, not for the Gods to foretell. Nadjia will find her own place when the time has come. So be it and it is so. Now let us feast and rejoice. Let us dance. Nadjia may not know her destiny, but we do know that her soul and Nardjol's have made the joyous commitment to journey together for this cycle upon the earth."

Chapter Four

NADJIA'S HONORING Ceremony had not been an occasion of joy for Damaya. "What a strange twist of fate that it was I who raised Olaya's daughter. I, who would have preferred that Olaya had never been born!" While the rest of the village rejoiced, Damaya, in the darkness of her memories, recalled the time of her sister's birth…

—⁂—

Soon Damaya would have a baby brother or sister. She could feel the excitement among the women in the village. A new soul entering the world was always a sacred event for the Tetwonee people. She didn't really know what to expect. Everyone kept telling her how lucky she was, so she figured it must be a very good thing. She remembered how excited she had been when her aunt made her a cloth doll wearing a beautiful and colorful ceremonial dress. When she had asked if having a new brother or sister would be as good as having the new doll, her uncle had laughed heartily and told her it would be much, much better. She couldn't wait! Women kept stopping by to check on her mother. Each time they did, they spent time with Damaya, giving her special attention and little treats to munch on. All this - and her new baby brother or sister wasn't even born yet! Though she figured things would get even better after the birth, she knew you could never be sure. Being happy with the way things were, she didn't want anything to change. She never forgot the day her grandfather left to go to town and never returned. She heard the talk about an accident in town that might not have been an accident, and some darker talk about townspeople resenting the Tetwonee way of life. She didn't understand it all, but she did learn that when you care about something, you must hold on to it tightly, or risk losing it forever.

Right now things were good and, being a practical sort of child, she decided she wanted things to continue exactly as they were. At first, it seemed that she might get her wish. But after a blissful week, the atmosphere abruptly changed.

People still kept stopping by, but now they spent less time with Damaya and more time with her mom. Instead of giving her treats, they gave her chores. "Damaya, be a good girl and help your mother. She needs to be resting." "Damaya, be strong and grown up. You have experienced six full seasons. It's not proper for you to whine for your mother. It's time for her to prepare to bring the baby into our world." Suddenly, it wasn't much fun at all.

It was a difficult time for her mother because the baby's soul was resisting entry into the world. Damaya was told to be brave as she was sent from her house to stay with her Aunt Raisha and Uncle Danior. Damaya was starting to wonder about this baby. She had thought it would make her life better, but instead it seemed to be bringing her only trouble. She hadn't liked it when her grandfather disappeared, but now she found herself hoping that her new brother or sister would disappear before it was even born. Damaya hated to be ignored and hated to be second to anything - particularly a baby that wasn't even here yet! She thought dark thoughts about the baby while sitting in her aunt's dwelling, and they got even darker when, several days later, she heard her mother's screams. She knew that women sometimes screamed in childbirth, but now all she could think of was that the baby was hurting her mother. Then and there, she decided she hated this baby.

She was awakened the next morning with news that the baby was born.

"Wake up, Damaya! Wake up! Your baby sister has chosen this time for her arrival! It's time for you to go back now and meet your little sister!"

Damaya glared at her aunt and pulled the fur covers over her head.

"Get up, Damaya. It is time for you to go home now."

Damaya emerged from under her fortress of blankets, glared once more, and stuck her tongue out for good measure before once again covering her head.

"Damaya, no more of these tantrums! Get up now or be dragged out of bed and paraded to your dwelling in sleeping clothes. Believe me, I have no more patience for this."

Damaya wanted to make enough noise so that everyone would hear it and know how unfairly she was being treated, but she recognized that edge in her aunt's voice. In the short time she had spent with her Aunt Raisha, she had learned to fear and respect that edge. Reluctantly she got up and prepared to return home.

"Remember what I say, Damaya. I know how much

*trouble can come from you. You will not share this trouble
with your mother. Your mother is in a time of rest and
quiet. Help is what she needs, not more problems." Raisha
continued to lecture her as she dragged a reluctant Damaya
back home. As soon as they got to the front of the dwelling,
Damaya pulled away from Raisha and rushed inside.*

"Mommy, I'm home! I…"

*"Shush, Damaya. Mother and baby Olaya are
sleeping." Adria, the village midwife, peered at Damaya,
disapproval radiating out of her still sharp eyes.*

"But…"whined Damaya.

*Adria's gnarled, wrinkled hands shook slightly as
she wagged a finger in front of Damaya's face. "No more.
You're the big sister now. Act like one!"*

*Damaya's eyes filled with tears as she made her way to
her sleeping area and sat there, alone and bewildered. She
curled up into a tight little ball and cried herself to sleep.
No one noticed.*

—m—

"Always you were the special one," she thought resentfully.
"Always you took what should have been mine. I did not
mourn your passing, Sister. But you are gone and I am

still here. So perhaps you did not get it all…" She left the festivities and made her way to her sleeping quarters to brood alone.

Chapter Five

THE SUN HAD long since completed its journey
across the sky and the moon was shedding its gentle
light upon the earth when Nadjia left the ceremonial
tent to return to the dwelling she shared with Damaya.
She felt light-headed, experiencing sensations of the
world spinning and tilting beneath her feet. Sometimes
she felt elongated and taller than a balo tree, with her
head hovering above the earth and her feet far below
her. Gandje had warned her that the ceremony would
leave her feeling not quite herself. He explained that
the ceremony had sent a part of her to travel the Spirit
Plane in order to retrieve knowledge from her soul.
She remembered very little, but he assured her that by
tomorrow she would feel fine.

Since her mother's death, no one had been able to use the Orb, and it was a good omen for the tribe that once again someone would have the skills of Far-Seeing and Healing - even if it wasn't yet known when her gifts would bloom or how she was fated to use them. She had expected Gandje to rejoice, yet throughout the ceremony he had been oddly subdued and somber.

As she entered her dwelling she was surprised to find Damaya waiting up for her. She took a step back, too weary to have to deal with Damaya's inexplicable moods. Today of all days, she had expected Damaya to be livid and cruel. Damaya had long ago made the naive assumption that her sister Olaya's honored place within the tribe was directly linked to her use of the Orb. For years she had nourished the dream that she would be the next one chosen by the Gods to use the Orb. Today her dream had been crushed.

"Greetings, Nadjia. I am sure you are tired, for much has happened in this Cycle of Sun and Moon. I must ask for your patience a moment longer. You see, Gandje has requested that I escort you to a place just outside of town and arrive before the Sun has started its journey across the sky. This unfortunately means that there will be little sleep for you tonight."

"But why, Damaya? He did not tell me anything of this. The townspeople do not much like us, and I do not like being anywhere near town."

"Yes, I know, but Gandje asked that I not explain until we get there. We must return to the village while the Sun is still in the first stages of its day's journey, so we must leave here well before the Sun awakens within the Earth." Damaya fidgeted, unable to look at Nadjia directly. "You know, Nadjia, Gandje spoke to me at great length. He is displeased with me for not opening my heart to you and embracing you as a true daughter. I'm sorry. Sometimes there is a rage-filled monster inside of me that reaches out to destroy anything or anyone that keeps me from getting what I want, or who has what I want. Sometimes I hate this monster and try to fight it, but alas… It is stronger than I. Do you think your mother's spirit is angry with me? I am frightened at times that she is. I tell her that I'm sorry. I hope she can forgive me." Damaya paused for a moment, a strange, feral look flashing in her eyes." Well, sleep child. You don't have long before we leave."

A few hours later, Damaya shook her shoulder

whispering, "It is time!" Nadjia groaned sleepily and rolled over. "Wake up," Damaya whispered intently. "We must move quickly and quietly so that we disturb neither people nor Spirits as we leave. Gandje was very specific in his instructions. You must do exactly as I say."

Reluctantly, Nadjia threw off her sleeping furs and pushed herself upright. Still disoriented from the ceremony, she grabbed her clothes, but then just stared at them as if seeing them for the first time. Finally, she managed to dress. Following Damaya's instructions, they crept silently through the village. Approaching town just as the Sun's glow began to awaken from its nightly rest, they heard the sounds of the townspeople setting up their wares in the marketplace.

"Come, Nadjia! Are you not curious to look upon these strange-looking people? See that pale thin man with hair the color of straw? Is he not interesting to look upon? And just look at all the wares he prepares to sell. Women use the things he makes to prettify themselves. They are highly prized. See how they glow? See the ones that are like little suns? It is said that when the Sun shines directly upon them, they capture its light and use it so that they too can sparkle and glow. Do you think they have strong magic in them? What hurt can come from us looking a little closer. Come!"

"I do not want to draw closer, Damaya. These people scare me. Can't we simply do what Gandje has asked of us? Something feels very wrong here."

"Soon, child. But there are things we must do first. Come. We must look upon these things of magic. Come with me."

"Is it this that Gandje wants us to do?"

"Hush, child. Don't ask so many questions. Just follow me."

As Damaya and Nadjia approached the stall, the man with the straw-colored hair glared at them. Nadjia timidly went up to him and gave him greetings, forcing herself to make eye contact as Damaya had instructed. She could feel Damaya leaning in toward her and heard her whisper, "Don't be afraid! I'll be back in just a moment." And with that she was gone, leaving Nadjia alone, frightened, and confused.

"So, what do you want?" The merchant didn't bother to conceal his contempt. "You can't afford my wares and anyway; you have nothing of value that I would want in exchange. So don't waste my time. Just leave now or I will ask the Enforcer to escort you out of town. We don't need your kind here."

Seeing him nodding to someone in the distance, she turned around and saw a big man wearing a look of authority coming toward her. She didn't know exactly what an Enforcer did, but she figured that this man must be one. His startlingly blue eyes glared at her.

"Well, well. Look what we got here. Aren't you kind of far from home? You lost or something, or just coming to town to make trouble? Well, whatever it is, you can just leave now. Come on, let's go." The Enforcer took her arm and began to lead her back toward the edge of town.

"WAIT!" Nadjia turned around and saw the straw-haired man's face twisted in rage. "Blasted animals - that's what they are! A necklace is missing! Either she or that other one took it. Search her, and if she don't have it, hold her anyway. One way or the other she's got something to do with it."

"Know what, Sam?" the Enforcer said in response, "They're none too bright either. Look what we got here!" He reached out toward Nadjia. "Girl, if you're going to steal something, at least try to hide it. Don't do you no good if it sticks out where all can see."

Horrified, Nadjia looked down and saw what appeared to be a bright shiny golden string sticking out from her robe. "That's not possible! I'm no thief! I don't know how this got here!"

"Sure, sure, we believe you. Of course you didn't steal nothing. The necklace just up and jumped into your pocket all by itself." The Enforcer laughed coldly as he grabbed Nadjia's arm. "Come along. Maybe a little time in our barred box will jog that memory of yours. What you did was awfully stupid. You really think that little golden necklace is worth losing your life over?"

Nadjia tried to shake the feeling that she had been transported into a dream world where nothing made sense. "Perhaps all of this is still the aftermath of the ceremony. Maybe I just imagined it was difficult to wake up this morning and this is all just a dream. Please," she pleaded, "let this be the Dream Time, and when I wake up I will go straight to Kora and ask for help interpreting these strange messages from the Spirits."

She was thrown into a small windowless room called a barred box. The door closed with a resounding thud, trapping her in total darkness. She waited to awaken from the dream. Frightened and confused, she felt even stranger than after the Ceremony of Power Transfer from the Orb to her. Finally she had to acknowledge that though this was a nightmare, it was no dream.

—∿—

Damaya made her way back to the village as fast as she could, knowing she had to get back before her absence was noticed. She could feel the Monster taking over but didn't care. All she could think was, "She's gone, finally gone. Now I can have what's mine." The demonic glint in her eyes gave her an almost inhuman appearance; the energy of the demon lent her speed and endurance. She approached the familiar outskirts of the village and quietly sneaked back into her dwelling. When the demon was upon her she felt powerful and invincible, but she knew that it needed to go back into hiding so she could complete her plan. As the monster receded, she thought of her sister and for a moment felt a pang of remorse, but quickly pushed it away, concentrating on what she must do next.

She waited a bit, then ran outside heading directly for Gandje's dwelling. She saw him staring intently off into the distance. As she turned in the direction he was looking, she saw a flock of pala birds and realized that he was studying them to see what message they carried with their flight. She waited impatiently for his focus to return to this world. Finally, as he began to return to the here and now, he noticed Damaya standing nearby. He spoke.

"The omens are not good. A time of trial awaits us." The faraway look had not totally left his eyes as he slowly turned and faced Damaya. "What's disturbing you, Damaya? Your spirit is not at peace."

"I've come to check on Nadjia. I wasn't worried when the Moon began its journey, for I knew she was with you, but when the Sun began its journey and still I did not see her, I was concerned."

Gandje's eyes snapped into clear focus. "What do you mean? She did not return last night? Is this what the omen portends? Come, we must find her!"

The Sun was preparing to return into the earth for its nightly rest, and the Moon was awakening to take its place, but still there was no sign of Nadjia. To the people of the village it seemed that she had disappeared without a trace.

Chapter Six

HUDDLED BENEATH his and Nadjia's favorite tree, Nardjol stared into space, his gaze unfocused. Every day of his life, Nadjia had been there. He could know where she was without even seeing her; he could frequently sense her moods by just closing his eyes and picturing her. Now suddenly he could feel nothing. When he tried to picture her he sensed darkness, yet felt her to be alive. He organized the men of the tribe to search for her, but they could find no signs. Still he refused to give up. He wandered for days and days, hoping that somehow he could feel where she was and be led to her. He wandered in the dense forest; he wandered near the caves since he had felt such a strong sense of darkness. He barely ate and barely slept.

An eerie silence descended upon the village. Gone was the light-hearted bantering and easy laughter that was the usual fabric of daily life. Hoping a ceremony would help shift the mood, Gandje called the villagers together to commemorate the end of the growing season and the beginning of preparation for the Time of Cold. He stood before them in ceremonial garb and lifted his arms up to the heavens. He encouraged their hopes, using his skills as a tribal elder to lift their spirits. He spoke of having faith and of the inscrutability of the Gods. The ceremony ended and he gracefully withdrew into his dwelling. Upon entering, he removed his robe and sank wearily to the ground.

After the ceremony, Nardjol once again sat beneath his favorite tree. His weary body hunched over as he fought the feelings of defeat that threatened to overwhelm him. Three days of purification and three days of asking the Gods to give him a sign - but still they remained silent. Anger crept into his eyes, hardening his resolve. He stormed off to his dwelling, filled his backpack and left the village. Practicing forbidden rituals, he brazenly sought guidance from the Gods. Making himself empty, he roamed the forest without thought, becoming nothing more than a vessel for the Gods. Momentarily, he became aware of a path beneath his feet - the path that led to town. Knowing that Nadjia was afraid of the town and would not go near it or the path that led to it, his surprise broke the sacred empty space, but he pushed all thoughts aside and returned to being a hollow vessel. His next awareness was of being spoken to roughly and rudely by a townsperson. Startled and frightened, he once again lost the sacred emptiness and immediately became filled with thoughts. All connection with the Gods was gone. *Nadjia would not come to town. She cannot be here. Am I so desperate that I grasp at any possibility to keep from the fear that she is truly gone? Perhaps Gandje is right. Who am I to question his wisdom? Perhaps it's time to return home.*

He turned to leave when he saw a young boy watching him curiously without the malice he saw in the others. Approaching the boy, he asked him if he had seen a young Tetwonee woman in town.

"When are you asking about? Ever? Or just the past few days?"

"The past few days." Nardjol looked at the boy hopefully.

"Well…" A townswoman ran up and grabbed the boy's arm, dragging him away. "Don't you speak to them. Do you hear?" The boy looked back and opened his mouth to say something else but his mother quickly dragged him away.

A large man introducing himself as the town Enforcer came up to Nardjol and gave him a look of disgust. "I think you better leave. We don't want you or your kind here."

"I will do so. But, I must ask. Has a young Tetwonee woman been in town recently?"

The big man leaned forward, towering over Nardjol. "I think I made it very clear. You need to leave and leave now or I will personally throw you out of town. Now, what do you think? Do you think one of your kind has been spending time here? NOW GO!"

The sacred emptiness was now replaced with a sense of dread. As the stress of his long ordeal, coupled with lack of food and sleep, hit him full force, he felt dizzy and crumpled to the ground.

The Enforcer grabbed Nardjol roughly, threw him over his shoulder and marched off, all the while muttering under his breath. Nardjol's next awareness was of hitting the ground with a resounding thud. The Enforcer dusted off his hands as he spat out, "Next time, I assure you, I will not be so gentle. Now go home while you still can."

Exhausted and temporarily defeated, Nardjol returned to the village and began to help with the preparations for winter. Still sure that Nadjia was alive, he stubbornly refused to give up hope.

Chapter Seven

ALONE IN THE DARK, Nadjia paced back and forth, hugging her arms to her chest. Remembering the Enforcer's terrifying comment about the golden string not being worth dying for, she began to wonder if they were going to leave her here to die. She sat on the ground moaning and hugging her knees until it hurt, relieved to be feeling and hearing anything to break up the vast and terrifying emptiness.

Time lost all meaning. Her stomach hurt, but she couldn't tell if it was from hunger or fear. Yet being only moderately thirsty, she supposed she could not have been there for long. The room had seemed pitch black and totally empty, yet she felt she was no longer alone. She saw, or rather sensed, a dim glow in the center of the room. Concentrating on it calmed her. The light grew, and so did her feeling of peace. She opened to the light and heard it speak to her. A wisdom and knowing from deep within told her to trust it.

"Greetings, Dear One. Sometimes adversity is our greatest teacher. Be not afraid, for out of the deepest dark comes the greatest illumination. In this time of emptiness you begin your journey. If only I could show you, but alas - there is no way. Find me inside of you, for that is where I abide. Feel the peace that comes of our union. Know that you are never truly alone. Know your power. Trust your gifts. Your soul is the soul of a healer and a knower. Always has it been so. Always will it be so. Remember, I am with you always."

The light faded but the peace did not. Nadjia knew now with absolute certainty that she would be fine. Her serenity increased as she remembered all that the Spirits had said to her during her Honoring Ceremony. She remembered their parting words:

"We send you blessings of love and strength and tenderness. We send you the blessing of Faith. These are the only tools you will need. Remember that these gifts are within you and therefore cannot be lost or taken away. Remember this even if you forget all else."

"Thank you. Thank you, Being of Light. Thank you for reminding me."

As she sat peacefully, filled with grace and faith, she was not surprised to hear noises outside the door. She was unafraid as it opened…

—⚙—

As the Enforcer opened the door, he was disconcerted by what he found. He expected a terrified, hysterical young woman. Instead, he found a woman possessed with an almost unearthly sense of peace and poise. Nadjia stood slowly and walked toward him. His first inclination was to take a step back. But as she spoke, he reminded himself that she was nothing more than a young Tetwonee woman. "I suppose it must be time," she said softly. "I'm ready."

She could still feel her connection to the Being of Light, and for that she was grateful. If the time had come for her spirit to travel beyond this body and this earthly plane, perhaps the Light Being would be her guide on the journey. The thought took away her loneliness and her fear. She carefully kept her thoughts away from Nardjol and home.

The Enforcer looked at her strangely and took her arm more gently than he had previously. He did not speak a word as he led her to a small building. As they entered, she saw several men, including the straw-haired man. One man sat apart from the others on a slightly raised platform. She wondered if he was their chief. She supposed that, like Gandje, he would be the one to decide her fate.

One of the other men spoke to the one she thought of as their chief. "I don't know why we're wasting our time, Joaz. She was caught with the necklace on her. Let's just hang her and be done with it."

"Patience, Sando. We are men of justice. Everyone here gets a fair trial. That's just how we do things here."

The one they called Joaz looked up at her as she entered the room. Still connected to the Light Being, Nadjia's perceptions were altered and expanded. As soon as she looked into Joaz's eyes, her soul recognized him. The recognition transported her to another time and place...

—⁓—

The bad men had grabbed his mother and many others from his tribe and were dragging them away from their homes. They were all chained together and he could sense his mother's fear even through her attempts to reassure him. Days had passed and he was tired and terrified. The men had not seemed so evil when they first arrived. They even spoke the same language as the kind men who could not even see the Spirits, yet tried to teach them about the spiritual world. Those men, who called themselves missionaries, had taken away a sickness that was hurting their people, and for that the tribe was grateful. Since the missionaries enjoyed sharing their silly stories, the tribe allowed them to do so and listened politely, as was right to do with a guest - even a misguided one. But these other men were different. They were evil.

They walked until they got close to the Big Water. Ahead of him he could see other people from other tribes also chained together and being forced onto a large, oddly shaped dwelling that seemed to have been built on top of the water.

As they got closer, a man who appeared to be their leader began talking to their captors. "This here's been a good haul - even more slaves than can fit on the ship. Take only the more valuable ones. Kill the rest. We can't leave until the tide rises, and we don't want no extra mouths to feed while we're waiting."

"But, sir. We don't have to kill 'em. Why not just let 'em go?" asked a young man with deeply penetrating blue eyes.

"Because we don't want no trouble. Besides which, they aren't much more than animals nohow. Not worth wasting your worries on. Just make it simple. Dispose of the ones we don't need."

The one they called "sir" walked along the line of villagers and pointed to ten of them, the small boy among them. "Get rid of these. They ain't worth nothing. Take care of it now." He turned his back and started to walk away. The blue-eyed one reached for a small strange-shaped object. He had a grim, haunted look on his face. Slowly, he and several others pointed similar-looking objects at the ten who had been chosen.

Just then a rain of arrows came out of the woods and the one they called "sir" was the first to die. A group of warriors from the tribe had been quietly following them. Unfortunately, these warriors had never before encountered guns. Within minutes, most of them were dead or wounded. The young boy's father had his knee cap blown apart. He was barely conscious as he saw his son being shot and killed. These men had shown his son far less respect than he would have shown an animal he killed to *feed his people.*

His soul cried out in horror. He saw his wife being taken away and his son die. His spirit lost its will to stay within his body, but leaving at this time was not meant to be his fate. As the spirit of his son left its body, he came to his father.

"Pau Pau," his son said, using the special name he always called him. "It is not yet your time to join me. I have a task to do. Mother has need of me, and in the between-time I chose to help her in this journey of our souls. It is something I must do for her. Do not worry, Pau Pau. I will be of greater service here than if I had stayed on the plane you currently inhabit. I will stay with her. She will experience much difficulty. But I will be there to help her through. We will both be fine." As the father felt the son touch him, he experienced an inexplicable sense of peace. He would live, for that was his destiny. But he never overcame the grief at losing his family in such an unspeakable manner.

—⧗—

Nadjia broke eye contact with Joaz. She felt disoriented, neither fully here nor fully there. "Pau Pau," she murmured softly, "the endless cycle continues." She shook her head and once again was in the present. She looked back at Joaz. He was pale and sweating.

"Joaz," said one of the men. "Are you all right? You don't look well."

"Yes…yes. I just had a moment of dizziness, but I'm fine now. Just give me a moment. I'll be fine." But he was not fine. For a moment, he had been a native warrior, watching his wife and son treated as if they were less important than the lowliest of animals. And when this young woman had called him Pau Pau, he knew exactly what that meant. No, he did not feel fine at all.

Joaz tried to pull himself together, but it was difficult to reconcile what he had just experienced with everything he believed to be true about the world. Sandoz was speaking, and he forced himself to listen.

"Joaz, you really don't look well. Why don't I take you home? Don't trouble yourself with the likes of her. Ain't worth our time and trouble nohow. Let's make this real simple. Let's just hang her and be done with it."

Joaz felt a stirring of rage unlike anything he had ever experienced. "Sir, you haven't changed a bit, have you? Have you no respect for human life just because it differs from yours?"

And just as suddenly as it had come upon him, it left. Once again he was just Joaz, and though he could remember it, the blending of the two realities was over. He felt exhausted and confused. Sandoz was looking at him with a look of concern and bewilderment.

"Just let her go. There will be no killing here today." Joaz put his head in his hands.

"But Joaz. We can't do that. It'll send a wrong message. She stole. We found the necklace on her; we can't just let her go. You said we were here to see justice done. That ain't no justice. That's just plain wrong."

Joaz sighed. He wanted to ask the young woman in front of him to tell her side of the story, but was petrified at the thought of looking at her or making any direct contact. He also knew that what Sandoz had said was true. He couldn't just let her go. It would make a mockery of the justice he'd devoted his life to. He looked at the men in the room, careful to avoid eye contact with Nadjia. "Today is not a day for an execution. She will be sentenced to ten years in prison." Now he steeled himself to look at Nadjia. "This is the lightest punishment I can offer for theft. At least you have your life. This time I'll not watch you die." He quickly averted his eyes. "We're done here. The Enforcer will take her to the county prison. They will leave immediately. I'm going home." He got up and left without a backwards glance. He had much to think about.

The Enforcer's attitude toward her had changed. He didn't understand it himself, but he now treated her with a respect bordering on deference. He felt that he owed this woman something. Nadjia understood as soon as she looked into his intensely blue eyes. In another time and space, he had been unwillingly responsible for her death. En route to the prison, they travelled together in a coach, yet neither of them spoke a word. On the fifth day they arrived in a big town. As the Enforcer handed her over to a man in a dark uniform, he looked at her and spoke for the first time. All he said was, "I'm sorry. I'm not even sure for what. I just know I'm sorry. I wish you luck." And with that he was gone.

Chapter Eight

PREVIOUSLY, she had never even spoken to a townsperson; now she lived among them. Her time in prison required adjustments on every level. Days were filled with seemingly meaningless tasks and there was never a moment of privacy. After a life of living in harmony with nature, Nadjia now spent almost all her time in buildings. It surprised her that townspeople could live their lives so disconnected from their souls, and she quickly learned to refrain from speaking about matters of spirit.

For some reason, the mention of anything beyond the immediate physical world threatened these people, and they responded with fear and anger. From her perspective, their view of reality was pitifully narrow, and it was difficult for her to respect their obvious willingness to fight to keep it that way. Learning that they resented anyone who was different, she learned how to speak and act as they did. But she never really fit in. Townspeople in general seemed to resent those who came from villages. Marnia, the warden, was one of the few who respected rather than feared Nadjia's past. Curious and eager to learn more about village life, she befriended Nadjia and, over time, helped her to assimilate. Nadjia and Marnia's differences were mainly on the surface. Marnia was short and plump, while Nadjia was tall and thin. Marnia's fair skin and fine yellow hair contrasted dramatically with Nadjia's dark skin and thick abundant hair. Yet they discovered much in common - including a deep curiosity about each other's culture. Marnia became the one person Nadjia could talk to about herself and her life in the Tetwonee village, and for that, she was grateful. Life in prison was hard, but not unbearable.

Her continuous bond with the Being of Light gave her a measure of peace. Over time, as her inner vision expanded, she frequently knew things without being told, and learned to subtly use that knowledge to help heal the spirits of others - prisoners and guards alike. She developed a reputation as a good listener - someone to go to when you felt down - eventually earning the respect of her fellow prisoners as well as those who worked at the prison. She did not like her fate, but she accepted it. During the day she was at peace and content with being able to help others. At night, her thoughts turned to Nardjol and her village, and her loneliness became almost unbearable. But always the Being of Light was present, giving her comfort and strength to get through the next day. After a while, she lost track of the cycles of time, no longer certain if she had been there for four full cycles of the seasons or five.

For Nadjia, the change began during the Time of the Cold, when each day seemed colder than the one before it. The food hall was frequently noisy and chaotic, for it was one of the few places where prisoners could interact freely with one another. But Nadjia had no interest in engaging in the meaningless chatter that usually went on. Marnia had not been to work in a long while, and Nadjia felt lonely.

When she heard that Marnia had returned, she was delighted - at least until she saw her. As Marnia shuffled into the food hall with downcast eyes, Nadjia sensed waves of despair emanating from her heart. She did not mean to pry, but the knowledge came to her that Marnia's daughter was quite ill and that their healers could do nothing for her. They were giving up, and feared that she would soon die. Nadjia knew better. She could see that the daughter's spirit was out of balance and hovering just above the child's body, but was not yet called to leave. She could also see dark energy residing within the body that could be treated with proper herbs and rituals to strengthen the body, thus allowing the soul to once again dwell peacefully within. However, if something wasn't done soon, the soul would not be brought back into harmony with the body and would depart. It was almost unthinkable to her that these people did not understand how to treat diseases of the soul, or even how to help a soul on its journey when it was called to leave its present body. Not for the first time, Nadjia was frustrated by her inability to help these people see past their narrow, limited perceptions. Her sadness and frustration were heightened by her inability to help her friend. Sensing that she was being urged to do more, she listened to that inner calling.

Cautiously, she approached Marnia. "Marnia, you

know that I am from tribal people, not city people. We have ways of healing that your people do not. I see that your daughter is sick. Please don't let my knowing this frighten you. It is simply from who I am. Sometimes I know things. Your people would call me a witch and think I was evil. My people would call me a Healer and treat me with respect. Our ways are very different. I have learned to keep this part of myself hidden, but you have been kind to me and I would like to repay you. I put myself in danger by sharing this with you, and I can't promise that I can heal your daughter, but there are things I can do that your healers can't."

Marnia regarded her with such sorrow and pain that it wrenched Nadjia's heart. "Nadjia, I have seen you help people when they are in trouble. But this is a deep sickness within the body. What can you do?"

Taking another risk, Nadjia answered, "Marnia, the sickness is also deep within her soul. That is something I can help. But only in a limited way." She hesitated for a moment, but then trusted her impulse to be more open. "I am a Healer, Marnia, and I could heal her soul, but if you brought your daughter to me and I did my rituals, I would be branded a witch and probably put to death.

Yet if you trust me, there are certain things I can instruct you to do that may help - but you must do them when no others are around. It is in proper balance for me to help you as you have helped me, but I can only do a little."

"Thank you, Nadjia. I understand and promise I will tell no one. Please, Nadjia. If you can help… I will try anything." Nadjia gave her some instructions. Though what she asked seemed odd to Marnia, she promised to go home and do exactly what she had been shown.

Three days later when Marnia returned to work, she went directly to Nadjia. "Nadjia, what you suggested has helped. The doctors are amazed that she is even still alive. Saura is noticeably better, but still very weak. Is there more we can do?"

Nadjia closed her eyes and sought out Saura's soul. Yes, she could see that now there was more life energy and better balance, but the body was still weak, and not enough healing and harmony had been created for body and soul to remain joined. "I am sorry, Marnia. The ancient rituals of my people might be able to save her, but there is nothing more I can do from here. Your people know things about healing the body that mine do not, but my people know things about healing the soul that yours do not. If your people and my people could be open and learn from each other, it would be a wondrous thing. Sadly, all that exists between our worlds is suspicion and fear. I may be able to teach you things that can help your daughter stay here a bit longer, but I cannot save her. Believe me, I wish I could do more."

Tears sprang to Marnia's eyes. "When my husband died, Saura was all that kept me going. If I lose her too, I don't think I could take that. It's just not fair! I…" Marnia turned abruptly and ran from the room.

Chapter Nine

IT WAS EARLY MORNING several days later when they came. "You're the one they call Nadjia?" the bigger of the two men asked. Nadjia nodded. "Come with us then." They took her arm and, without another word, led her to a small room. It was cold and sparsely furnished with two uncomfortable-looking chairs, an old beaten-up table, and one small dirty window. Her taciturn guards offered no explanation. "Wait here," they said. She heard the sound of the door being locked as they withdrew.

At first the fear was a small voice, easily controlled. As the Sun rose higher in the sky, the fear grew. Despite the light that filtered through the window, the grim room reminded her of the time she had spent in the barred box. Once again she drew courage and comfort from her connection to the Being of Light. Finally the silence was broken by the sound of voices outside the door.

"Hrmmph! I don't know how you convinced them to give their approval." The gruff male voice sounded agitated. "I still must say this is most irregular. Are you sure you want to go through with this? I'm really not so sure I like this. Most irregular…"

Nadjia could hear a soft voice replying but could not make out the words.

"Foolish. It's all quite foolish, if you want my opinion. But it's out of my hands now. The decision's been made. I hope for your sake that it's the right one."

The door opened and a small man anxiously twisting his moustache entered, accompanied by none other than Marnia.

"Hrmmph! Most irregular. Well, so you're Nadjia?" He peered at her through his thick glasses, his hands fluttering nervously. "I suppose you look harmless enough. Still, I don't like this one bit. Hrmmph! Well, there you are. It's been done. I suppose you two should be getting along. Hrmmph! Don't like this, really don't like this. Well, too late now. Nothing to do but get on with it. I hope you know what you're doing." Without further comment, he turned and walked out the door, muttering to himself as he left. "Hrmmph! Most irregular, but that's just how it is…" The muttering became softer as he continued walking.

Marnia looked at her shyly, then began talking nervously. "I'm sorry you had to spend so much time waiting, and I suspect that the guards didn't bother to explain. You see, even though you're only a little more than halfway through your prison time, I convinced the judge that you should be released now because you're such a model of good behavior, and I promised to look after you and to take responsibility for you. I told them that I needed someone to help me take care of my daughter and I wanted it to be you. They feel sorry for me because I lost my husband and they know my daughter is very ill, so I guess I used that a bit to convince them to do this for me. You told me you could help my daughter if you were free to perform rituals to heal her soul, and now you can try and in turn I can do something for you too. I can give you your freedom."

Nadjia paled, frown lines creasing her brow. "Oh Nadjia, I thought you'd be happy! Don't you realize what this means? You're free! I'm hoping you'll come home with me and try to further heal my daughter, but you're free. You can go home!"

"I have often imagined this day - the day I became free - and I am grateful to you. Certainly l will try to help you. But going home will not be so easy. All l know is that I travelled in a coach for many days to get here. I have no idea how long I traveled or from what direction. Do you remember when I asked you once about my records? You told me that they do not say where I came from or what city I was first arrested in. You see, Marnia, I don't know where home is. I only know that it is far from here. I fear that I cannot go home."

"I'm so sorry, Nadjia. It's true that there is no record of where you came from. It only says that you arrived with an Enforcer from a small town. He never stayed to fill out the papers. I'm so sorry." Marnia fidgeted awkwardly and stared thoughtfully at the floor. Suddenly a smile brightened her face as she looked directly at Nadjia. "Nadjia, you can stay with me. I'll take care of you and find work for you. You'll see. It'll be all right. We'll make it work."

"Yes," said Nadjia softly. "Yes. I'm sure we can make

it work. But first, let's see what we can do for Saura."
She sighed deeply, adding even more softly, "I miss my
people, but at least this will be a better prison."

"Nadjia, how could you say that? Don't you
understand that you are free?"

"I'm sorry, Marnia. I didn't mean it that way. Of
course, I am very grateful. It's just that here in town there
is so little connection to Nature and Spirits, and I miss
my old life. What you have done is very generous, but I
am afraid I will feel trapped here in town. You are right,
though. We will make it work."

That night Nadjia did a ritual for Saura, allowing her
full power and gifts to flow freely for the first time. As
she knew would happen, Saura's soul and body became
steadily healthier and more balanced. Saura healed,
blossoming into a strong and vibrant child. And so began
the next phase of Nadjia's journey.

—⁓—

Marnia found Nadjia a job in town, and as the years
went by they became as close as sisters. People
respected Nadjia and came to her with their troubles.
But always she had to keep hidden the source of

her knowledge. It was difficult to live among people who were so frightened of the spiritual world, and she frequently found herself judging them for their ignorance. Without her spiritual understanding and her connection to the Light Being, she would have found her life sadly disappointing and her loneliness intolerable. Instead, she lived in a state of gratitude, confident that she was exactly where her soul meant her to be.

Lately she had been having vivid dreams. Even without Kora, the village Dream Woman, to help interpret them, she knew that a blessing was to come to her in the guise of a chance encounter. With these dreams came a sense of excitement and anticipation.

Chapter Ten

HIS JOB WAS FINISHED, but unlike the last time, he felt no frantic hurry to get away. He strolled down the street toward the diner, enjoying the sights and sounds. His attention was drawn to a woman running in his direction. She was an attractive young woman in her mid-twenties with long dark hair. As she drew closer, he found himself gazing into dark eyes that radiated power and depth, eyes that stirred something deep within him.

"Excuse me, sir. What brings you from your small town to the city? You do still live in that town, don't you?"

"I must beg your pardon, miss, but have we met before? It would not be like me to forget a beautiful young woman, but maybe you have me mixed up with someone else? I don't think I know you - but we could fix that real quick." His blue eyes were playful and flirty as they looked into her dark ones.

"It's not like that, sir. There's no way you could recognize me, for I barely recognize myself." She sighed. "I am the Tetwonee woman you brought to this town - but that was before the passing of many cycles of the seasons," she said, slipping into her old style of speech. "You left me here without saying where I came from, and I have been unable to find my way back home. But, you know where that home is. Will you take me there?"

He just stared for a moment, trying to collect his thoughts. He began speaking slowly and hesitantly. "You know, it happened some time after you came here." He paused, then continued. "But times got real tough back home. There was a cold season that was the coldest anyone could remember, and then the rains just never came. The crops withered and died, and the people and animals had nothing to eat. Joaz - you remember him? He governs the town and acts as judge and just about anything else we need him to. Well, anyway, he saved us. He gathered everything we had that we didn't need for survival and put it on wagons. Then he sent a bunch of us to travel real far to find cities that had food we could barter for. Nobody would've given a thought to your people - we just wanted to survive - but Joaz did. Let me tell you, it didn't make him real popular. Once we had enough to know we would survive, he insisted that some of us go with him to your village and make sure your people had food too. Everyone grumbled pretty loudly, but he wouldn't hear it and just kept insisting. Finally, there wasn't no other way but to bring food to the village." Nadjia nodded and silently thanked the spirits. She waited as the Enforcer stood gazing at her with an odd look on his face. "When we got to the village, well… um…you see…it just wasn't there no more." Seeing Nadjia's stricken look, he hastened to add, "It wasn't like they all died or nothing, they'd just moved on. I mean, there was nothing there. Everything was gone, so we figured they moved somewhere they could find food and water. We looked around some, but there was no sign of nothing. They moved, and wherever it was they'd gone to, it had to be pretty far away. There wouldn't be no place nearby that had water or where they could find food. Believe me, we knew that the dryness spread real far. I'm sorry, miss. They're gone and they ain't never come back."

Nadjia was sure this was the chance encounter her dreams had foretold, but it was not as she expected. The dreams had been bright, not dark. Was this meant to tell her that she should just accept her fate and find happiness where she was? Unbidden words came to her lips, and she stepped aside to let them be spoken.

"Sir, I thank you for your story, and I thank Joaz for thinking of my people. Would you please take me back home?"

"But miss. Didn't you hear? There ain't no home left. And it's a long ways. Looks to me like you got yourself a life here. If you leave, it won't be so easy to get back here."

"Still, I will go home."

Chapter Eleven

GANDJE WORRIED about Nardjol after Nadjia's
disappearance. His concern mixed with displeasure when
he discovered that Nardjol had tried finding Nadjia by
invoking the help of the Gods through a state of trance.
The realm of the Gods was the work of Healers and Holy
Men. It was dangerous territory for the uninitiated and
untrained. But Nardjol was not Gandje's only worry.
The omens foretold hard times ahead, and there was
much work to be done in preparation. He kept Nardjol
particularly busy, partly so that he would have no
more time for foolishness, but also because he believed
that work would help him heal from his loss. He was
unsuccessful on both fronts. Nardjol, feeling the presence
of Nadjia in his heart, had no intention of stopping his

"foolishness." Though he refrained from requesting that the Gods lead him again in forbidden trance, he felt compelled to find Nadjia. Each night he said prayers, asking the Gods for guidance. The Gods were silent, but his faith persisted.

The Gods and Spirits had spoken truly to Gandje, for the village was indeed experiencing hardships. Nature was capricious and at times could be cruel. This was one of those times. The cold seasons were colder than usual and the wet seasons were drier than usual. Food was scarce. After three full cycles of abnormal seasons, Nature's moods became ominous. First, she withheld all her warmth and sent only bone-chilling frost. Then she withheld her water and refused to send the rains. The animals moved away or died, and the growing things withered. No ceremonies would appease her. Finally Gandje determined that the land no longer wanted the village to remain on it. They must move or they too would die.

It was a sad time. The villagers did not know where they would go; they only knew that the land refused to sustain them. Gandje made it clear that once they left, they would not return. This was particularly difficult for

Nardjol. The last of his hopes were being shattered. Now if, by some miracle of the Gods, Nadjia returned, she would no longer be able to find them.

The villagers allowed Gandje to lead them, secure in the knowledge that the Gods would lead Gandje. They traveled for almost a full cycle of the Moon. When first they sensed moisture in the air, they grew hopeful that they had found their new home. Still, Gandje pressed on. Arriving at a narrow pass between green hillsides, Gandje stopped and closed his eyes, nodded, and continued on. When they came out on the other side of the pass, they encountered an old man standing calmly, resting on a large staff. The villagers were uncertain what to do, but Gandje just smiled. The old man stepped forward.

"Welcome. I have seen you in my dreams and knew this to be the time of your arrival. It is as the Gods have foretold."

"Thank you, Brother of my Spirit. The Gods have spoken truly. You are the one they showed me as well." Gandje bowed his head respectfully. "You are a blessing for my people."

"As are you, Brother of my Spirit. It will be a blessing for both our peoples. The Gods sent sickness during the last time of cold, and many died. We who survived are few, but now once again we will be many. Come. Let us rejoice. "

And so the two tribes became as one, and there was much rejoicing. A young woman had her eye on Nardjol and it was assumed that they would become mates, but Nardjol did not want any woman but Nadjia. The Wise Men of both tribes spoke with him. "Let Nadjia go," they told him. "It is not fitting for a young and healthy man to refuse to become a mate and father. Is not Behia lovely to look upon, as well as skilled in crafts and cooking? Is she not a light spirit who smiles readily and is gentle in speech and manner? Is there something about her that is displeasing to you? If there is not, then it is only proper that you take her as mate." Nardjol could not refuse, but his spirit was heavy.

As the time of their union grew closer, Nardjol knew he could not betray his love for Nadjia. A great darkness descended upon him. He remembered what had happened to Damaya shortly after Nadjia disappeared. An evil spirit took possession of her. She did strange things and spoke words that made no sense. Shortly thereafter, her spirit fled her body and few mourned her passing. He wondered if a similar evil was trying to possess him. He returned to his dwelling with a heavy heart, murmuring softly, "Gandje, please forgive me, but I must break my promise to you. I cannot let Nadjia go. I know I must try to find her - even if it means again engaging in forbidden ritual. It may be that I have taken leave of my senses, but I am compelled to do this."

Nardjol had watched and studied all that Gandje did before and during rituals. He told himself it was out of respect, but perhaps he was being less than honest with himself. He understood more now than when Nadjia had first disappeared. This time, when he fasted and purified himself, he added additional rituals that he had observed. He was not afraid; rather he felt supported and guided. At last he was ready to again become nothing more than a vessel for the Gods. Before opening himself to being possessed, he added one last and dangerous ritual, which included drinking a cup of broth made with sacred herbs.

"Please, Gods, hear my plea and lead me to Nadjia. Help me to find her," he pleaded, as he emptied himself of all that made him Nardjol.

—∞—

Nardjol lost all track of time, but then what did time matter? He was hungry, but that was merely a concern for the physical form that he occupied at the moment and was ultimately of little importance. His name was…sometimes he didn't know. He understood now that this name was merely a label that he had for this particular phase of a much larger existence. He held in his mind an image of a woman. Sometimes he couldn't remember why, only that he had to find her. And he walked and he walked and he walked…

Chapter Twelve

MARNIA WAS WORRIED. "But Nadjia. What will you do? If your people are no longer there, what will you do? Please stay. We are family. Don't go off on a quest that makes no sense."

Nadjia was not worried. "It is my destiny. My spirit is calling me to do this. To fail to listen to one's own spirit is a form of death much worse than the separation of spirit from body. I will be fine, more than fine - for I am whole - my body and my spirit are as one. Please don't worry, Sister of my Heart. We have been connected many times throughout eternity, and will never be truly apart. You have given me so much. For that I will always be grateful. We have danced our dance in this earthly passage, and it has been a fine dance. When we meet again, it may not be in this cycle of life, but it will be a joyful reunion. I will hold you and Saura in my heart always." They embraced. Nadjia's eyes were brimming with tears as she went to say her farewell to Saura.

The return trip was very different from her journey away from her home. On both occasions, her future was uncertain and unknown, but this time, strengthened by adversity and supported by her connection to the Being of Light, she was possessed of unwavering faith. She radiated peace. Whatever happened now was unimportant. She was already at home - at home within herself.

On her way back to the village, there was no conversation between Nadjia and the Enforcer, for Nadjia had little she wanted to say, and the Enforcer was at a loss for words. This woman made him uncomfortable in ways he did not understand, and he did not have much interest in trying to figure it out. Silence was fine with both of them.

They completed their journey back. He offered to escort her to the site of her old village, but she declined, saying she wished to go alone. He was relieved. Having said their farewells, she walked slowly out of town, down the path leading to her old life.

—◆—

As sometimes happened, the Being of Light's presence became very strong and she felt herself slipping into a light trance. With each step along the path, more and more images from the village arose in her mind. Most were quite pleasant; some were not. The darker ones had to do with the loss of her parents and with Damaya's betrayal. Her spirit sorted through them, helping her come to a place of peace with her past. The strongest images were of Nardjol, and they lingered while all others slipped away.

The forest began to thin, alerting her that she was close. She did not know what she would find, but knew that resonance from the past would remain, even though the village itself was gone. Her trance state deepened. She did not question this. A deep trance would make her a tool of the Gods. She surrendered to their whims and felt a further strengthening of her connection to the Being of Light. She trusted this Being completely. Without its presence, she would have withered. Through it she had found her power and her peace. Through it she had gained wisdom and compassion. A deep quiet settled upon her. Her mind became empty and her heart full. Once again, images of Nardjol formed in her mind. She stepped out from among the trees and onto the land that had once been her home.

The images became stronger, and she sensed Nardjol's presence. She imagined him sitting against their favorite tree under which they had shared so many happy moments. "Oh, Nardjol," she thought. "Time has not been gentle with you." She sensed grief radiating from his heart. To live fully, one's spirit must be aligned with and wholly inhabit one's body. This was not the case with Nardjol. His spirit was losing its connection to this world. There was something not right with him and she suspected that, in his desire to find her, he had been delving into matters forbidden to the uninitiated. Death would come to him soon if he did not receive healing. Worse than death, if in dying he did not properly disconnect from his present form, his soul could be left to wander the Netherworlds - unable to return. If this happened she could lose him forever.

"Dear Nardjol," she spoke aloud. "Do not let your grief destroy you. I see now that you have need of me. Know that I will always love you. It is neither the time nor the place for your soul to depart. Have faith. We have been together many times and will be so again. Accept with grace all that your soul asks of you in this cycle. Hardship can destroy us or strengthen us. The choice is always ours. Let it strengthen you. Find peace."

She reached to the Being of Light. "You have been my constant companion and never have I asked anything of you, but now I do. Please tell me what I can do to save Nardjol. I fear he is dying. Never before have I healed someone who was not present before me, never before was I capable of doing so. I open myself to you. I care not what price I pay or what it takes from me to do this. I must heal this man." Tears ran down her face as she reached with the strength of her desire to connect with and touch the man she loved. She hoped she could reach him through trance. She knew that this task would demand great power, and she was not sure she could do it. She also knew that it was a task full of danger. If she was not careful, she too could become lost outside of her body, doomed to wander the Netherworlds, unable to return.

The figure beneath the tree opened its eyes and gazed upon Nadjia, giving her hope that she had indeed reached him. The figure began to speak. "The Gods were silent for so long, but now they allow me to gaze upon you. You are so beautiful - even more than I remember, dearest love. I became impatient and asked the Gods to lead me, even though Gandje forbade it. I could not do otherwise. One last time I went into forbidden trance and allowed the Gods to guide me. But now I am weak. My soul wanders and I am unable to return it fully to my body. So, here is where I die. But now my eyes feast upon you one last time, and my death shall be filled with peace. I walked in trance for longer than can be imagined, forgetting more than I ever knew. I saw dimensions of existence that most never see, and experienced that all of us - no matter how different we may seem - are one and interconnected, both here and in other times and places. How sad that now that I understand so much and could help so many, it is too late. I die now, and my newfound wisdom dies with me.

"But all is not lost, for now that the end is near, I get to see the two things nearest to my heart - you, dear Nadjia, and this…" He reached out his arm, pointing to all that was around him. "…the place of my birth and of my happiest memories. At first I thought the Gods had abandoned me. For as soon as I found myself back in the village, no longer was I an empty vessel. I was myself again. Just Nardjol - alone, weak and hungry. I asked myself: Do the Gods want me to die here, or have I perhaps just lost the ability to remain in trance? But, I could not have lost the trance, for how otherwise could I be seeing you? I know myself to be close to death. Perhaps, after all, the Gods have granted me my wish. I die with a vision of you in my mind and I die in this place I love above all else. It seems right that my body's final resting place shall be the old village. Death must be near, for I am rambling on and on. Ah, but the mind can indeed play strange tricks on us. Almost could I believe that you are here in the village with me in reality - not just in the eyes of trance."

Nadjia stared - her eyes widening in utter disbelief. "Can it be true? You are truly here in the old village? I thought you were a vision. Never did it occur to me that you could be here in the flesh. The Gods led you here? We are not meeting in trance?" Understanding what had taken place, Nadjia again felt tears running down her cheeks - this time tears of joy.

"Nadjia, dearest Nadjia, is it true? You are not a dream? Can it be so?"

She raced across the field and threw herself into Nardjol's very real and very solid arms. "I am real! We are here together! The Gods have reunited us! This is not a vision and not a trance. I can heal you, Nardjol - you will not die. I will bring you back into harmony with your body." Nardjol, realizing that she was indeed real, hugged her tightly, joy replacing grief in his heart. They gazed at each other in wonder, each feeling the fullness of their spirits as their hearts overflowed with gratitude.

They shared with each other all that had taken place during their time of separation and rejoiced in the miracles that had brought them back together. Nadjia helped Nardjol to heal, eager for him to regain his strength so they could make their way back to the tribe.

The Being of Light radiated with delight. Wholeness and harmony were restored. Nadjia and Nardjol would go on to become leaders to their people, spreading joy and healing to many. Her task here was done.

BOOK THREE

BOOK THREE

Chapter One

"NAOMI, COME AWAY from that window. You've been gazing out of it all morning and the others are already arriving. I would have thought that after eighteen years you'd have outgrown your fascination with the view." Sarita shook her head. "I've helped raise your mother and I've helped raise you, and I can honestly say I've never known two more accomplished daydreamers."

Unfolding her tall slender body, Naomi removed herself from the window alcove. "Tell me another story about Mother. I never even got a chance to know her - or for her to know me - and yet I miss her so. It's unfair that she died so young." She sighed deeply, pushing away the feelings of longing that always accompanied thoughts of her mother.

"Not now, child. There's no time. You need to finish getting ready. Besides, I've already told you too many stories."

"Actually, Sarita, you haven't told me enough. And Father won't talk about her at all. I want to know who my mother really was. I don't like feeling as though she is a woman wrapped in mystery." Naomi grabbed her hairbrush and finished brushing her long, thick blond hair. "Oh, please, Sarita. Just one more story." Clasping her delicate hands together, she playfully pleaded with her beloved nurse.

Sarita frowned as she glanced out the window, glaring accusingly at the Temple buildings that seemed to command so much of Naomi's attention. Still, she had to admit that the morning sun reflecting off its tall, slender white towers was a spectacular sight. At this distance, it was impossible to make out the details of the artistically placed trees and shrubs, or the beautifully manicured gardens. Even so, the structure emanated peace and tranquility. She tore her own fascinated gaze away and focused on getting her young mistress off to her lessons. "Brother Thomas tells me that you daydreamed through your mathematics lesson again. Dearest, how are you going to run the District Estate if you don't know your numbers well enough to check the books? You need to be concentrating on your studies."

"I know you're right. But that's assuming I want to do what Father and everyone else have decided for me. It's all just so...so...well...It just doesn't feel right! There's more to life - more to existence - than this. It feels stifling and..." she struggled for the right words "...just so incomplete. I know that doesn't make sense. Sarita, am I crazy? Sometimes I really feel like reality isn't real - or at least that what we call reality isn't all there is."

"Shush, Child. You have too vivid an imagination. Keep your feet planted firmly on the ground and your head out of the clouds. You have no understanding of how difficult life can be. People depend on the District Estates, and your family helps run the District. Where's your gratitude? You could have been born to a family that lives on the streets. We don't always get what we want, but you have been given quite a bit. You've been blessed. So stop griping, young lady, and appreciate what you have and what it allows you to do for others. Don't be selfish.

"Naomi," Sarita continued, "forgive me for lecturing

you, but human nature is flawed and man must always fight his inherent selfishness. Our society isn't perfect. We haven't created utopia, but we've come a long way. The Districts and the Temple are reflections of that. Have you forgotten all that you've learned of our history?" Her loving gaze softened the reprimand behind her words. "Remember, child. There was a time when we were a self-centered and savage civilization. In our narrow-minded ignorance we believed that wealth and power were to be revered above all else. Those who were the most ruthlessly power-hungry became leaders, using power as a means of control. They foolishly hoarded more material goods than they could possibly use, leaving others underfed, uneducated, and in poverty. This couldn't last, and eventually society collapsed, bringing chaos and darkness to all. In that time of darkness there came a sacred shifting in consciousness, and the higher values of man began to take precedence over the lower instincts. Those who helped bring about this shift in power became the creators of the Temple. Generations later, they built the beautiful structure you find so mesmerizing. The original founders of the Temple Order understood that leaders must first and foremost be people of integrity and humility, willing to put others' needs before their own greed and self-interest. In the time of darkness, the Temple Initiates assumed temporary control of society and took upon themselves the power to pick leaders. Though many qualities are required of a good leader, the one they would not compromise on was purity of heart.

"Later, when power was given back to the people, the Temple kept one power for itself. To this day, Temple leaders have the right to elevate someone to leadership or to remove him. Three times in my life, I have seen them request that the leadership of a District not be passed to the rightful heir. Each time, the person was respectfully given another task, but was denied power over others. The system has worked. Some argue against the inheritance of positions of power, and others believe that all members of society should be equal. Perhaps they are right. We still have a class system, but at least in our district, all are fed, all are educated, and all have adequate clothing. The Temple supplies healers who are available to all. The elderly can stop working and be well provided for. New mothers are supported and encouraged to stay with their children until they reach school age. Each District makes sure that its people's basic needs are met.

Each District's Estate has enough land to grow abundant food, and enough facilities to make whatever goods are needed. Each District is ruled by fair and just leaders. You've been born to a ruling family. For generations, it has been the privilege of your family to manage this District's Estate. The system works because its leaders are willing and able to put the needs of their people above their own. There's no room here for petty self-interest. So now, young miss, hurry along or you'll be late to your class. And no more feeling sorry for yourself!"

Sarita did not like withholding information from Naomi, but she would do as she was told. Sarita was a nursemaid, as was her mother before her. It was not her place to question the decisions of a ruling family, yet she would do anything and everything she could to love and protect this child.

Chapter Two

NAOMI'S DISTRICT was the largest one in the territories and included the entire province of Nanchon and a small section of Tarychon. The District was made up of twelve Great Houses, and the task of governing the District was divided among the twelve families that made up those Houses. Naomi Sarton's family made up the thirteenth Great House, and it fell to House Sarton to lead the other twelve. She had no siblings or other family, so when her father stepped down, the responsibility for the District would fall upon Naomi's shoulders. She had been only a few weeks old when she lost her mother, and her father never remarried.

All the children of the Great Houses met at the Great Hall once a month for special tutoring. Although the purpose was primarily educational in nature, a great deal more was accomplished. The thirteen families used the opportunity to socialize and deepen their bonds of friendship and trust. The adults used the time to discuss the functioning and wellbeing of the District; the children received instruction on their eventual duties. The tutors were all Temple Initiates, and this was an opportunity for them to remind future leaders of higher values as well as to observe and get to know them better.

By the time Naomi arrived at the Great Hall, most of the thirty-nine students were present. As usual, until the arrival of the tutors, discipline was lax and the students laughed and shared stories with their friends. As soon as Naomi entered, David caught her eye. She watched his face light up. He approached her, warmly took her hands and led her to where he had been sitting, all the while sharing his latest news.

"My father is letting me take over more and more of the responsibilities for House Tarklin. We are opening a new facility this month, and now provide work and sustenance for over forty families, as well as supply all the cloth and leather used in the District. I see that you too are becoming more involved in the governance duties of House Sarton. Ah, Naomi. I know you so well. Most are thrilled when they reach this point in their lives, but you are not content and still long for something else. You've been this way for as long as I have known you. But perhaps that is part of what I adore about you." David laughed easily. "Always be prepared for the unexpected around you." Becoming more serious, he continued. "Do you think you'll ever be at peace with your duties and your role? You know that I would like nothing more than to spend the rest of my life with you. But I love you too much to ask you to be other than who you are. You have a restlessness in you and I would not ask you to settle down until you're ready. I'm willing to wait for you for a long time - but not forever. Someday you'll have to decide and give me an answer." David returned to his easy smile. "Don't look so glum, Naomi. It doesn't do a guy's ego any good when a woman looks glum when he speaks to her of marriage. Don't worry, I'm not asking for an answer today. I'm just letting you know I haven't changed my mind. Come on. Let's go join the others. House Milltane will be hosting the yearly District dance, and they're coming up with some wild themes for it. They're asking the other Houses to help with the decorations. Let's go hear what they're planning. We don't have much time; the Temple tutors will be here shortly."

Naomi went with David and joined in the conversation with the others, but her mind was not at rest. David was right. She would have to make decisions about her life soon. There were just so many unanswered questions, and so much that didn't make sense. As they went to their first class of the day, her heart was heavy with confusion.

Chapter Three

THE TUTOR'S VOICE was like a distant drone until she heard her name being called. "Naomi, perhaps you have a better solution for this problem?"

Naomi, her attention suddenly brought back to the present, stuttered out a response. "Ple... Plea...Please forgive me, Brother Franklin; I'm afraid my attention wandered for a moment. Could you repeat the question?"

"If you thought your wandering lasted only a moment, then your sense of time needs as much sharpening as your focus. Would you like to share with us where you went in your wanderings?" Brother Franklin's voice betrayed his thinly veiled irritation.

Aware that the question was rhetorical, Naomi tried to remain respectfully silent but failed miserably.

"Actually, I was pondering some questions of my own - ones I believe you have answers to." Despite her feeble attempt to stop it, the floodgates opened, and years of frustration and unanswered questions poured out. Her eyes blazed with challenge as she looked directly at Brother Franklin. "Can you tell me why the Temple keeps much of what it teaches its Initiates secret from the rest of us? And why I'm discouraged from asking such questions?" She sighed. "There is so much I want to know - things that go far beyond what you're teaching us in this class; things that touch upon the Unseen and upon the Sacred Energies." Once again, challenge sparked through her eyes. "The Unseen Energies surround all of us and are an integral part of who we are. I also know they play a large role in healing. Opening, balancing, and expanding these Energies leads to greater emotional and intellectual clarity, and more robust health - even if a person is not ill to start with. So why aren't we encouraged to understand these Energies? Why aren't we taught ways to open and expand them?"

Brother Franklin realized that the conversation was moving into delicate areas, and wished it was not taking place in the middle of his class. He thought it best to cut the conversation short and talk with Naomi privately after class. He tried unsuccessfully to divert her. "If you're quite through, we can finish this conversation later. For now, let's return to…"

"But I'm not through! The only thing I'm through with is being put off every time I try to talk about these things. You and I both know that other dimensions exist - in addition to those we see with our physical eyes - just as we know that Energy exists even though we can't see it. Yet the Temple discourages exploration. Only Initiates are taught sacred meditations and spiritual practices that expand perception and provide access to alternate dimensions. Why? Obviously, having greater vision and access to greater knowledge is important in the work of healing, and can clearly make someone a more effective teacher. It would follow, therefore, that it could also make someone a better leader. The Temple wishes us to be wise, just, humble leaders, so why not teach us these techniques? I already know of their existence, so why continue to discourage my curiosity?" Naomi's voice and eyes made no secret of the anger and frustration she was feeling. "I've heard all the stock answers. I don't agree with them. I want to - no, I NEED to - understand more about these sacred Energies and about other dimensions of existence."

The tension in the room was palpable as the other students watched to see how Brother Franklin would react. Wanting to lead the discussion away from topics of the Unknown and restore calm to the room, he projected an aura of tranquility, slowly soothing the disturbed Energy flow. As the Energies in the room regained a sense of balance, he continued. "It takes courage to challenge the status quo. Backed by wisdom, it is a great quality in a leader. A curious mind can be an asset, but also a source of endless frustration. Can you not be content with your place here? You have a position of significant responsibility. You are more than capable of fulfilling your duties and being of great service to the District. You live here..." he pointed to the ground "…with your feet planted in the physical world. Don't keep reaching beyond it; it will only confuse you. We each do what we can to help others and to be of service. You must learn to accept your destiny."

Naomi was not satisfied. "Now comes the lecture about curiosity being dangerous. This is where you tell us that attempts to connect with Other Planes or dimensions of reality are perilous and should not be attempted. Rubbish!!! I believe that ignoring them is dangerous." The frustration that she had kept at bay for so long broke free. "Don't you understand? It is not I who reaches for the Beyond; it is the Beyond that reaches to me. I sense things around me but can't always comprehend what I sense. Sometimes I see things when I look into someone's eyes. Sometimes I know things they haven't told me or that haven't yet happened. Last week I wanted to tell the cook to watch over and be more protective of her child. I had a sense of danger and an image of wheels. The next day, the girl ran out into the street and was run down by a carriage. Now she's paralyzed. Maybe I could have prevented this tragedy, but I was afraid to say what I'd seen. I am told that my curiosity and longings are merely signs of selfish discontent. Everyone keeps telling me I should remain in a state of ignorance and just do what I'm supposed to do. But I don't know that I can. Can't you understand? I see things and know things!" She glanced wildly around the room with a strange look in her eyes. Her penetrating gaze stopped at young Clara. "Take Clara, for instance. She's sad right now and feels suffocated by her mother, who will not give her enough space to make her own decisions. You could counsel her and her mother and it would help some. But the deeper problem is now in Clara. Her heart is tentative and she no longer trusts herself. Opening the Energies that are blocked around her heart would enable her to feel her anger toward her mother. Facing this frustration and anger and being able to express it would help her find her own strength. It would lead her to being a happier, healthier person. Somehow I also know that this is not the first time she has experienced this. She has encountered it in other places and other times, and in personalities other than Clara - the personality she is known as now. I know these things. I can see them. But you want me to ignore them and focus on keeping the books and making sure the District runs well. I may have the ability to do so, but I don't have the heart for it." Naomi had been thinking these things for as long as she could remember, but had had no intention of blurting them out before all her classmates! Feeling the beginnings of tears, she ran out of the room to save herself further embarrassment.

By lunchtime, word of Naomi's outburst was the main topic of conversation. After a brief conversation with his superiors in the Temple, Brother Franklin rearranged the rest of his schedule and set up a meeting with Naomi's father. The situation had gone far enough and was getting seriously out of hand.

Chapter Four

THE MEETING was to take place in the conference room just off the reception hall of the Temple. Jonathan Sarton had been there only once before, and the memories were not pleasant ones. The bitterness and resentment that he typically kept under tight control threatened to overwhelm his usually poised exterior. Brother Franklin saw the discomfort reflected in Jonathan's eyes.

"Jonathan, I know this is difficult for you, and I'm sorry, but the situation can no longer be ignored. It simply must be dealt with before it becomes potentially dangerous. Please, I hope you'll try to work with us for the best of all concerned - in particular, your daughter. We're not your enemy."

Jonathan, straightening his shoulders and pulling himself up to his full six feet five inches, cut an imposing figure as he glared down at Brother Franklin, his eyes like sharpened daggers. Brother Franklin returned his glare with compassion, for he could see through the anger to the seething pain that had still not healed. He sighed inwardly. This would not be an easy meeting. They walked down the hall in silence, each lost in his own thoughts. Brother Franklin thought about the meeting ahead; Jonathan found himself transported to memories from the past…

—⚏—

They were in love. Jonathan had walked on air for weeks after Bethany agreed to marry him. It was hard to keep his mind on his responsibilities when his thoughts kept drifting to images of her long blond hair cascading down her graceful back, and the twinkle in her blue eyes. He found himself contemplating how the delicate features of her face were in contradiction to the strength of her personality, when he should have been focusing on the reasons for the sudden tensions between House Sarak and House Perloti. But he didn't care about a few lapses here and there. He was happier than he ever believed he could be.

The wedding was exquisite, and when Bethany became pregnant six months later, they were euphoric. Nine perfect months of marital bliss - and then the problems started. At first they made jokes about pregnant women and their moods, but Bethany was experiencing more than just moods. They feared it was an emotional breakdown, and when she awoke in the middle of the night, babbling incoherently about things that only she could see, they brought her to the Temple. That was the day Jonathan's perfect life ended.

Two days later, Father Jerome, the head healer, requested a meeting with Jonathan. When Jonathan entered the conference room, Bethany was there, but not as he had ever seen her. She seemed so small and vulnerable. Her head hung down as she stared at her hands, which were clenched tightly in her lap. With effort, she raised her head. Their eyes met. Hers were red and puffy; his grew dark and angry and filled with fear. Preparing himself for the worst, Jonathan was surprised when the first words he heard were: "Your wife will be fine." When this pronouncement was followed by a long pause, Jonathan returned to fearing the worst, holding his breath until

Father Jerome finally continued. "However, spontaneous spiritual awakenings of this magnitude have been encountered only twice in the entire history of the Temple. We know that she does not feel a call to Temple life, but if she does not learn how to work with and control what she is experiencing, it will drive her insane. If it opens too far before we step in, we will not be able to help her."

At first Jonathan wasn't sure if he should be relieved or terrified. "Then you can help her? She will be OK?" Once again, there was a long delay. Impatiently, Jonathan demanded, "Is there more to this that you haven't yet told me?"

Father Jerome looked directly at Jonathan. "We can help her, but it's not that simple. It takes time to learn to control these things. The first time we have a record of this happening, not enough was done and the person later lost his sanity. The second time, the individual was taken under Temple tutelage and was fine. In fact, he went on to become a great Healer."

"But, it has not progressed too far yet, right? You said she can learn to control it, so that's what you'll do, isn't it?"

Jonathan did not like the sound of Father Jerome's sigh. It sounded too much like a harbinger of doom. "Yes, *we can teach her. But this is not an easy thing to do. It may take years, and she will need to be in the Temple while she learns. My son, chances are she will not be able to just control it and shut it down. If that is the case, and we believe it is, she will have to become an Initiate and spend her life in the Temple. We know this is most unusual. Sometimes people want to come to the Temple but don't have the needed abilities, so we must turn them away. Occasionally someone may show some abilities, but has no interest in Temple life, so we help the person shut down what is awakening within him. Never do we seek people out. People come to the Temple only when they're called. Initiates want to be here more than they want anything else in their lives. With Bethany, her spiritual powers are very strong. We can't just shut them down. She must be trained to use them."*

Jonathan's head was spinning. "Are you saying she must leave me and live in the Temple? What of our marriage? No Initiate can be married to a non-Initiate. And what of our child? Are you saying that our child will be born in the Temple? This isn't right. This isn't possible. It can't be happening!" He turned to Bethany. "This isn't what you want, is it?"

Father Jerome placed his hand on Jonathan's shoulder. "Son, I know this is difficult. Your wife has made her decision and has asked that I explain it to you. There are very few choices here. If she's not trained, she'll go insane. We can slow the opening down and keep it under control, but only for a limited time. She has agreed to go with us to the Temple. We have agreed to help her stay at home with you until the baby is born. We can't promise this, but we believe it will be possible. Once the abilities open to a certain degree, she must leave - no matter when that happens."

"So, she'll have our baby and then abandon it? And me as well? I don't understand. Why must she leave? Why can't we stay together?"

"Jonathan, you know that even though not all Initiates live within Temple walls, Initiates cannot be married to non-Initiates. And since no non-Initiates are allowed to live in the Temple - not even children - Initiates having children must take only those assignments that allow them to live outside of a Temple. Their children are always brought up integrated into society. You cannot live within the Temple; due to the intensity of Bethany's awakening she must live within the Temple. You will have to raise the child on your *own. We have never encountered a situation like this, but there's simply no alternative."* Father Jerome paused, trying to gauge Jonathan's reaction. *"I know this is a lot to take in, but there's more."*

Jonathan felt that a dagger had been plunged into his heart. He didn't believe he could take any more. He looked at Father Jerome, his face crumpling and a hollow expression in his eyes. *"What more can there be?"*

"What has happened is an extremely rare occurrence and it would be better if people didn't know that it's even possible. The Unknown is not something to explore casually, and it's safer to keep people from thinking about such things. I know this may be hard for you to understand, but it would create unnecessary problems if this were to become common knowledge. Sometimes people have emotional problems that look like spiritual awakenings. The spread of this knowledge might cause some people to assume that serious psychological disturbances are signs of spiritual awakening, and fail to seek proper help and healing. It would be prudent on many levels if this knowledge didn't spread."

Jonathan was furious. *"First you tell me I'm losing my wife, and now you order me not to tell anyone? I think people will notice if she's missing, particularly if she's not here after the baby is born."*

For the first time, Bethany spoke. "Jonathan, I'm not happy about this, but I understand the necessity. You didn't experience the nightmares. I can't live with them. Something must be done. I don't mind people not knowing the truth. They wouldn't understand, even if we tried to explain, and I don't want people to refer to our child as the one whose mother was strange and had to be taken away. For the child's sake, as well as for the Temple, we don't have to share this. We'll tell people that I'm experiencing difficulties with the pregnancy and that a Healer from the Temple will be coming to stay with us. After the delivery, we'll tell everyone that I'm weak and possibly dying, and that we don't want any visitors. Then when the time comes, you'll tell people that I'm near death and have been taken to the Temple for treatment." Her eyes filled with tears. "I love you more than words can say. If there were any other way, I'd take it. It's not what I want, but it's my destiny. Whether I want it or not, what I have been given is a gift that I can use to help many. I don't want to leave you with false hopes. I doubt I shall ever see you again. This knowledge is also a part of what is awakening in me. I want to believe that I can remain with you and our child, but, most likely, it is not to be. My dearest love, don't fight it. It will only make the situation more painful for both of us. Let's enjoy the time we're given. I'll always love you - that will never change. Please, don't make this more painful than it already is. I don't think I could handle that. Lie if you must, but let me believe that you'll be fine and that you'll make sure our child will be well taken care of. I will try to follow his or her life from afar."

He saw Father Jerome staring at him. "Is there more you want to say? I think I've heard all I can handle for one day."

Father Jerome nodded. "There is one more thing you should know. We have no record of this happening to someone who is pregnant. We will want to monitor the child carefully."

Jonathan surprised them all with his reaction. "I'm not sure I'll agree to cooperate. I suspect that you're not telling me the whole story and that there are other reasons you want this to remain secret, reasons that are very important to you. I could go along with what you're saying and not tell anyone the truth. But I demand something in return for my silence. I'm losing my wife. I feel like I'm losing my life. Promise me that I'll not also lose my child - that he or *she will not also end up being taken to the Temple. You tell me that some who request admittance into the Temple are refused. If my child asks, you will refuse."*

"Jonathan, what you ask is most irregular and potentially dangerous. We can't make agreements to refuse someone if they ask to be an Initiate and if they belong in the Temple."

"It's also most irregular to force someone to enter the Temple against their desire. You want me to keep an important secret for you. I have my price. Give me your word."

"Son, you're feeling great grief right now, and this has all come as a shock. Take a moment to think it over. You don't want to give me an ultimatum about your unborn child. You don't even know what this child will be like."

Jonathan was too consumed with grief to be reasonable. He was drowning, and needed something he could hold onto, someplace where he felt he had some say over what was happening in his life. Bethany understood and decided to throw him a lifeline. She spoke up. "This is my child too, and what you ask of us is painful beyond imagining. I side with my husband. Make this agreement in exchange for our cooperation. It's our price for silence."

Jonathan looked at her with gratitude. Not so much for what she had said, but because she understood. Now they were a team, standing together against the world. He felt a measure of control and with it, his first inkling that he might actually survive this ordeal.

Father Jerome looked from one to the other. "I see that neither of you will budge. Can we not take some time to think this over? I believe..."

"NO!" Jonathan interrupted him. "I've taken all I can. You will agree to this request. There is no more compromise, no more giving in me. I need to know that at least I will not also lose my child." Father Jerome looked from Jonathan's grief-ravaged face to Bethany's sad and determined one.

"It seems that I have no choice, though I believe this is a decision that we will all come to regret. It is done. You have my word. I will instruct any tutors who work with your child to focus away from Temple business and to stress to him or her the importance of the child's destiny as an heir to House Sarton. I believe Sarita, your nursemaid, knows something of what is going on? Can she be trusted with this knowledge? If so, she should attend Bethany at the birth. However, it would be best if a Temple healer and

the nurse were the only ones attending."

Bethany looked grateful. "She can be trusted and I would like very much for her to be there for me. Thank you."

Jonathan was brought back to the present by the gentle pressure of Brother Franklin's hand on his shoulder. "We're here, Jonathan. Are you ready? They're waiting for you."

Chapter Five

JONATHAN WAS HAVING trouble breathing. The last time he had been in this room, he had lost his wife, and Father Jerome had been the one to break the news to him. He had not realized that Father Jerome would be the one in charge of this meeting as well. He fought to gain control against the feelings that were threatening to overwhelm him.

"Thank you for being here, Jonathan. I know this is difficult for you, but there are things we must face and must discuss."

Jonathan struggled to be calm but could not contain the storm of emotions swirling in his heart. "Is Bethany still alive? I still don't understand why I had to lose all contact with her. That day you brought me here, there

...let me see you just one more time and tell you that. You're one of the few and Initiates who even know that some of our Initiates live in seclusion, separate from the world. I can say no more. You know that. Please, Jonathan. Don't let your emotions cloud your reason. We must speak about your daughter today. You can't ignore what is there for all to see. She is pulled to the Temple and at some point will ask permission for entrance. We have not encouraged her in any way. We have upheld our part of the agreement and will continue to do so. An agreement - even one that should not have been made in the first place - is sacred and we will not break it. However, be aware that it may not be only Naomi who will suffer, but the entire District as well. Left where she is, she can spread seeds of discontent. People don't feel secure when they're ruled by a leader who doesn't want to lead. If she's willing, she'll make an excellent leader. Because of that, we will grant you six months. At the end of that time, she must either graciously accept her role, or we shall remove her from the line of succession and give the leadership to someone else. I'm sorry, but at this point there are no other options. If I were you, I would let her make her own decision. Use these six months wisely."

Jonathan was not given much time to decide how he wanted to handle this. Still caught within the storm of an old wound, freshly opened, he returned home to find Naomi waiting for him in his study. Curled up in his favorite overstuffed chair and dwarfed by its size, she looked more like a little girl than a young woman blossoming into adulthood. He wanted to rush to her, take her in his arms and protect her from the pain and complexities of the world. It saddened and angered him that he could not shield her from life's wounds. He didn't know what to do or what to say, so it was a relief when Naomi began the conversation.

"I suppose you heard about my outburst today. I guess everybody has by now. I'm sorry. You must be terribly disappointed in me. I'm so confused! Throughout my life, I've been trained and prepared to take my place in the District. Everyone has constantly reminded me that this is my duty and my responsibility, and that I'm blessed to be in this position. I've been told so many times how lucky I am and how grateful I should be for these opportunities I have. Over and over again I hear that I will make a great leader, and how fortunate the District is that I'm your heir. Every time I even think of deviating from this chosen path -or should I say, this path that has been chosen for me - I'm reminded that I'm being ungrateful and selfish. Father, is it so wrong to want to realize your heart's desire? I don't want to run the District. I want to study in the Temple. It's what I've wanted ever since I can remember and it's all I want. David wants me to marry him and I believe I love him.

But, when he asks me, all I can think is that marriage to him would mean having to give up being in the Temple. There are two things that I want desperately, and I fear that they may be mutually exclusive. I want to go to the Temple and I want your approval. My happiness is in your hands, Father. Is it possible that I can have both?"

For the second time in one day, Jonathan felt like he couldn't breathe. It seemed that the nightmare was repeating itself, and he didn't think he could survive it happening again. All rational thought abandoned him, leaving him adrift in a sea of emotions.

"You said you were confused, so let me give you some clarity. You have responsibilities to the District. Whatever your personal discontentment may be, it will stay that way - personal. You will never again give any outward signs of not wanting to lead. If you do so, you will be considered unfit to govern. If you want my approval, you'll put aside any foolish notions of running away from life, and you will fulfill your duties here."

Devastated, Naomi replied, "What do you really know of the Temple that you can say such a thing? Becoming an Initiate is not about running away from life - it's just the opposite. It's about devoting yourself to parts of life that most people are ignorant of and afraid of. So who's running away? Most people run away from the knowledge that there is more to life than what they see with their eyes. Did it ever occur to you that it is everyone else who is running away and that the Initiates are the only ones brave enough not to? You're asking me to deny what I feel and what I know to be truth. You're asking me to live a limited existence, cut off from a large part of who I am. The problem is that I can't disappoint you. I know how painful it is for you to have lost Mother, and I would rather die than add to that pain. I can see that you've never recovered and I know that's why you've never remarried. I can't ask you to also lose me. I will try, Father, but, I fear that one of us must lose me. If you don't, then I will lose myself. But I'll try."

Jonathan sat looking at the empty chair long after Naomi left. He had won, but it felt like a hollow victory.

Chapter Six

THE NEXT COUPLE of weeks had a dreamlike quality to them. Naomi went through the motions of life, but it was as if someone else now inhabited her body. At least her body's new occupant had "proper" instincts. Unlike the "awake" Naomi, this one always seemed to respond and to smile at just the right moments and - at least on the surface - to be very content with her life. When people asked about her outburst with Brother Franklin, she smiled and made light of it. The conversations and speculations about it died down and people moved on, looking to entertain themselves with more exciting news. Her decision was made. She would disappoint herself rather than her father. Though aware that she would have to turn away from her dreams and aspirations, she had not expected to also feel empty and deflated. The only way she could get through her days was to numb herself to the pain and disappointment. Unfortunately, the human psyche does not allow for one area to be numb while the rest function normally. Closing off any aspect of life, be it joys or sorrows, inhibits the vital life force. Naomi was learning something about the sacred Energies she was so curious about, just not what she had wanted to learn. She was learning about the effects of denying them free expression. Determined to protect her father from pain, she ignored her own. Such decisions always come with a price.

There was one person who saw through her charade. David's love for her was pure and unselfish. This allowed him to see her for who she was, rather than who he wanted her to be. He knew that if Naomi continued on her current path, she would give up her dreams and accept her life as a governor of the District. He also knew that if she did so, she would most likely become his wife. He loved her beyond measure, but realized that he would rather lose her than see her lose herself and be so unhappy. Wanting time to talk with her alone, away from the stresses of other people and their expectations of her, he invited her to spend a day in the countryside with him. He knew a beautiful spot near a cascading waterfall. It was the perfect setting for a picnic lunch and some much-needed conversation.

Chapter Seven

"WHAT ARE YOU trying to do, Naomi? You may be fooling your father and you may be fooling the District, but I don't buy it. People don't change overnight. You're not happy and you're not being true to yourself. How long do you think you can go on pretending?"

"Oh, David. What choice do I have? Father's not as strong as he looks. Sometimes I think he's barely able to hold himself together. Something happened to him when he lost Mother and he's never fully recovered."

"I know you love your father very much, but maybe you're worrying too much and trying too hard to protect him. Don't you think it's time you also took care of your own needs? You know I adore your father and would do anything to protect him from harm, but I think he's strong enough to take care of himself. Certainly he can't want you to be miserable while pretending that you're happy."

"David, it's not that simple. You know that I can sense things about people that others are unaware of."

"Like what you said about Clara and her mother when you were talking to Brother Franklin in class?"

"Yes, exactly. No matter how strong my father appears to be, I can feel a place of deep pain, resentment, and confusion within him. It's like a wound or a crack in his armor that makes him fragile. He's strong, but he's also weak. I love him deeply and owe him the honor of loyalty, but it's also more than that. I have this strange feeling of being responsible for him - as if I'd wronged him in some way."

"Wronged him? That's absurd. You've been the most devoted of daughters. How could you think such a thing?"

"I want you to try to understand this - which is asking quite a bit because I'm not even sure I understand it. You remember what I said about Clara having experiences in other dimensions and as personalities other than Clara? Sometimes I'm afraid I'm crazy, but I sense that kind of stuff about people. I know I've been a good daughter. But if other dimensions of experience also exist, isn't it possible that somehow, somewhere, we have interacted in roles other than as loving father and daughter, and that I have mistreated him? As weird as all this sounds, the bottom line is that it's really important that I don't hurt him again."

David didn't totally understand, but he accepted what he heard. "These feelings you're talking about, are they part of the reason you want to study in the Temple?"

"In some ways, but that's not all of it." Naomi sighed. "I don't even know where to begin."

David smiled. "Why don't we begin by having lunch? I think you need something to cheer you up. We can talk more after we eat."

She looked at David with gratitude. "David, sometimes I think you're the only one who understands me and the only one I can talk to. I really do love you. I wish life weren't so complex and that I could just agree to be your wife. I'm so sorry that you have to be caught up in my confusion. I want to marry you, but it's just that…"

"I understand. I wish I didn't understand, and that I could just pressure you to give up your 'foolish dreams and confusions' and badger you to marry me. I know that you have decisions to make and that you have to do what's right for you. I don't want you to marry me knowing that you would be unhappy as my wife. Over time we would both come to regret it."

They set up their picnic lunch in silence, each lost in their own thoughts. Slowly, conversation resumed. At first, they chattered about inconsequentials, but by the end of the meal Naomi began to share things she had never before put into words.

"When I'm with you, I feel at peace. Mostly it's because you're at peace with yourself and because you don't want or expect me to be anything other than what I am. I think that should be the definition of true love. Father loves me, but wants me to be something I'm not. It's not just his words that tell me so." Naomi paused as she grappled with how to explain these concepts. "This Energy that the Temple talks about - I know it's real. I can see it and feel it. I can see that Father has darkness around his heart. It's like a vortex that pulls in Energies around him. He feels empty in the place that used to be filled by Mother, and so he tries to fill the void with other things. Unfortunately, one of those things is me. Do you have any idea what that's like? When I'm around him, there is this Energy current that pulls at me. When I let him pull on my Energy, he feels better and his pain lessens. He interacts with people all day long, and the more full he is, the more Energy he has to give others. When he feels good, the people he encounters also feel good - or at least better than before the interaction. When he's in pain, the other person may feel drained by the encounter and not know why. I don't know if this makes sense to you, but I know we're all intimately interconnected. Our Energies swirl around us, affecting everyone we come into contact with, and through them, everyone they come into contact with. So, I help my father and, in the process, become a center of Energy that indirectly helps the entire District." Naomi looked embarrassed. "You must think I sound arrogant and self-important, claiming that my sacrifice is noble. Perhaps you're right and I'm just overprotecting my dad and afraid to disappoint him."

"No, Naomi, not at all. I neither see nor feel these Energies, but what you're saying is fascinating. If we influence what goes on around us, it makes sense that the strongest among us would become centers of power that can affect the rest of us either positively or negatively. I guess we should all start taking more responsibility for what we think and feel."

Naomi nodded. "If I'm right, the thirteen Great Houses make up a kind of Energy center. When we function well together, we help the District in ways not seen with the eyes. Perhaps my most important task could be to become a positive center of Energy that keeps a balance within the District and between the Great Houses. When I think of it that way, the job doesn't seem so onerous. It does, however, feel unbearably lonely. It's not a responsibility one should have to take on alone. I keep seeing images of what it could be like to do that kind of work within a group of people who all understand the importance of working together Energetically."

Chapter Eight

RUTHLESSLY SUPPRESSING any doubt or sorrow about her decision, Naomi devoted herself to the governance of the District. On the surface all seemed well, but as the months wore on and she continued to deny the essence of who she was, her health began to suffer. There were days when she felt tired, but ignored the fatigue and pushed through with her responsibilities. Often she'd feel out of breath, with small exertions leaving her with her heart pounding, and almost gasping for air. She ignored this too. She was becoming an expert in the art of being unaware of herself. It started with her practice of ignoring her emotions, but had now progressed to physical symptoms as well. When she fainted after walking down a flight of stairs, she could no longer ignore her condition. She finally shared with her father what was happening. Immediately, he asked the Temple to send a Healer.

The Healer, an older woman called Mother Clarita, asked Naomi many questions. After a thorough examination, she laid her hand over Naomi's heart and then left the room without further explanation. Naomi wanted to ask her what she had found, but felt too tired to call out to the woman's retreating back. She promptly fell asleep and began dreaming. In the dream, Mother Clarita soothed her and told her to relax. After that, she was suddenly marrying David - yet he didn't look like David. Though they were happy, she was frustrated by his lack of spiritual awareness. The dream shifted as she discovered to her horror that she had killed David's father, except that when she saw the body it wasn't David's father but her own father. The dream shifted again and she found herself looking into the face of love - but was unable to see distinct features as they continually morphed into new faces. Finally, all the images blended into a single ball of brilliant white light, and a great peace settled over her as she drifted into a deep and healing sleep.

While Naomi slept peacefully, Mother Clarita conversed with her father. "She is meant for Temple life - why do you still deny her this? I see that your heart is still sorely wounded, but the blame is misplaced when you direct it toward the Temple. We did not create the awakening that Bethany experienced. We merely saved her sanity and her life."

"I didn't invite you here to discuss my wife. What's happening with my daughter?"

Mother Clarita looked at him for a moment before answering. "She's dying. In physical terms, her heart is giving out. The same could be said on the spiritual and Energetic levels. She no longer has the heart for living the life she has committed herself to. She has chosen death over disappointing you."

Once again Jonathan experienced the terrifying sense of being unable to breathe. As always, it was caused by his struggle to lock down his emotions. Seeking release, long-buried resentments rose up in the form of irrational feelings. "You've already stolen my wife and now you come here trying to steal my daughter! I'll not have it! I won't lose her to the Temple!"

"Then you'll lose her to death," Mother Clarita said

matter-of-factly. "You're not being rational. Jonathan, please calm yourself." Mother Clarita went to him and placed her hand lovingly on his forehead, sending forth a burst of sacred and healing Energy. "You know that what you're saying is the pain speaking. No one stole your wife from you and no one is trying to steal your daughter. Think about your daughter. Think back through her life and see her as she is - not through the haze of your pain around losing Bethany. Think back to the day when she agreed to put aside her dreams of the Temple. Relax and think back to that day." She kept her hand on his head as she softly and rhythmically spoke to him.

Gradually, Jonathan relaxed and felt the storm of panic and pain recede. As he did so, he remembered the exact words his daughter had spoken on that fateful day: *"The problem is that I can't disappoint you. I know how painful it is for you to have lost Mother, and I would rather die than add to that pain."*

"NO!" Jonathan wailed. He felt like his heart would break yet again. He thought about losing his daughter, and about having lost his wife. Allowing himself to feel the full force of his pain, he finally and fully grieved Bethany's loss. Mother Clarita held him while he sobbed and wailed.

She was not concerned by the intensity of his outburst. On the contrary, she knew that once he released the pain blocked around his heart, he could finally heal. Perhaps it was not too late to also save his daughter. It took several hours for the storm of emotions to abate. Once it did, Jonathan knew his course of action. Afraid that he might lose his clarity or change his mind, he wasted no time in acting upon it. He looked at Mother Clarita and for the first time in many years felt no resentment toward a Temple Initiate. He had forgotten what it was like to feel a measure of peace within his heart.

"I've been a fool for too long. I suppose I should thank you for helping me to come back to myself - though I can't say that the last few hours were exactly a picnic." He managed a wry smile. "Please come with me. There is something I need to do, and I believe you should be there."

They entered Naomi's room as she was awakening from her restful sleep. She smiled at her father and looked questioningly at Mother Clarita. Jonathan rushed to his daughter and took her into his arms. "My dearest, precious daughter. I hope you can forgive me. I've been a fool, and a blind one at that. You told me that your happiness was in my hands and I threw it away. As your father, I gave you life, but that doesn't give me the right to control what you do with that life. You are who you are, not just an extension of me. I see now that your heart desires the Temple above all else. I give you my blessings if that is the life you truly want." He smiled, yet sadness could still be seen in his eyes. "I love you, and I'm sorry I have been so selfish with that love. I'm sorry that it had to come to this for me to see clearly. It seems that I'm destined to lose you one way or the other. Your heart is ailing and in need of healing. I believe that Mother Clarita would be willing to take you to the Temple, where they can tend to you. When you are well, perhaps you can begin your training as an Initiate."

Mother Clarita was watching her closely. "Is this what you truly want? It will mean leaving all that is familiar to you. It will mean a life of discipline and study, and it will mean devoting yourself to service. Are you ready to make such a commitment? If so, you will need to meet and speak with Father Bernard. If he agrees, you will spend six months in training and study. Then, if your entrance is approved, you will become an Initiate and dedicate your life to the Temple."

Naomi looked hesitantly at Jonathan. "Father, are you sure? I keep having a feeling that I've stolen your life from you before, and I can't stand the thought of doing it again. I'd do anything to keep from hurting you."

"Shush, child. You'll follow your destiny, and I will learn to accept mine. You've stolen nothing from me - only given me great joy. If anything, it is I who have stolen from you. I freely give it back. Stop worrying about me. I'll be fine. I promise."

Naomi felt as if a great weight had been lifted from her chest. She hugged her father, tears of gratitude soaking her face and his shirt. When they finally pulled apart, she looked at him and smiled, happy in the knowledge that the pain he had carried within his heart for so long was finally on the mend.

Chapter Nine

AN ORB OF LIGHT - lightness free-floating in space. Other orbs - twelve in number. Others? Confusing, since orbs and space were one and the same...

"Who am I? What am I? What is 'I'?" she screamed in terror. Must cling to selfness - hold on to individuality. Otherwise, all is lost. All? What was there to fear losing? Don't go there; danger lies in that direction. Oblivion. Stay where it's safe...Fear and doubts assailed her, bringing pain in myriad forms. The discomfort was a balm and an anchor. Worry - growing in the fertile field of uncertainty - soothed her. Relief spread through her being. Now she knew. She had purpose and direction. Her purpose was to relieve herself of pain. Slowly she relaxed and felt better... The control slipped and once again she found herself back

in free-floating space. Ecstasy washed through her being.
Peace consumed her. Relaxing her efforts to stay bound, she
once again felt the boundaries between self and otherness
soften. Fear of the unknown and unknowable...If I am
not 'I', then what? The thought invited pain to again rear
its head. To her vast relief, she sensed that worry, fear and
pain were reasserting themselves. Once again, she had
purpose. And so the cycle continued...

—⟁—

Naomi awoke with a start. In the morning light the
dream seemed harmless, so why was her heart pounding
and her body covered in sweat? As she had been
instructed to do in the Temple, she reached for her
journal, recording the dream while it was still fresh in her
mind. She looked around her. Such an odd sensation to
find herself once again in her father's house, waking up in
the room she had slept in every night until the time she
entered the Temple. She thought back through the past
seven months...

Once her father had given her his blessings, her heart
had felt light and free and Naomi had healed quickly.
When the time came, she was ready for her introduction

to Temple life. There had been twenty-two candidates in her group. On day one, they were reminded that there was no guarantee that any one of them would be accepted into the Temple at the end of the six months, and some might decide on their own that this was not the life for them. Each day began early with prayers and meditation, followed by breakfast. The rest of the day was divided into segments, each beginning with meditation and followed by classes, study and various forms of physical exercise designed to enhance spiritual growth. Meals were eaten silently; the candidates encouraged to spend this time in quiet contemplation. By the end of the day, they gratefully fell into their beds. While most of the exhausted candidates eagerly looked forward to their one day off, Naomi spent her free day studying and practicing the exercises and meditations - all the while still hungering for something more. She hoped her ambition meant that this was the life for her, but as much as she loved her time in the Temple, she could still sense a longing for something undefined. She supposed it was this yearning that got her to where she was now.

Utterly certain of her path when she started, she later surprised herself with doubts. "Doubts are not bad," they told her, but how could she interpret it otherwise, considering that they told her this as they were sending her home? They said she was peeling away her outer self, breaking through the shell that made up her false self in order to uncover her true self. But what if she didn't have a "true self?" What if she reached her inner core and discovered that there was only unfulfilled longing? What if the reason they had told her to take some time away from the Temple was that she was too flawed to become an Initiate?

Twenty of the twenty-two initial candidates had been accepted and were already taking their vows. One had been rejected and sent home. Naomi, her status undefined, was told to go home for a minimum of seven weeks, or until she knew her path with absolute certainty. The delay only seemed to be exacerbating her doubts. Perhaps they saw something in her that she herself had missed. Perhaps they doubted that Temple life was truly for her. Father Jerome's last message to her had insinuated that if she returned to Temple life, she might be sent to a region far from home. He suggested she take time to explore her current life and see if she could truly give it up. Were they purposely trying to discourage her? If she said she wanted to go back, would they even accept her?

   She looked out her bedroom window, remembering how much of her childhood had been spent gazing at the Temple with longing. Was it still what she longed for? Was she ready to go from being heir to House Sarton and a future District ruler - a position of power and freedom - to being Sister Naomi, a role in which she did only what she was assigned to do? She didn't even know to what position she would be assigned - assuming they accepted her. No one had spoken to her of her strengths or her desires. No one had asked her if she wanted to be a Teacher or a Healer, or if she had an interest in working in the gardens. Heaven forbid they thought she would make a good Temple administrator and planned to put her behind a desk! Their only instructions as they sent her home were to find inner peace, ask her heart to illuminate her path, and not return until she felt certainty. What kind of certainty did they mean? She didn't believe her doubts were deep enough to keep her from wanting to return. It seemed somehow unfair that they were putting her into this situation. So what if she was enjoying her old life? So what if she had unanswered questions? She still craved the life of a Temple Initiate -

why couldn't they just let her take her vows and be done
with the questioning?

Having the rest of the morning to herself and being
in no rush to face the day, she continued to stare out the
window at the Temple. During her time there, she had
been given a new perspective on life. Hopefully, it was
one that would help her find the clarity she was searching
for now.

"What kind of person am I, and what do I want
from life?" she asked aloud. She sighed. If she was going
to have a conversation with herself, perhaps these were
not the questions to start with. The answers were not
to be found in her definition of herself. She had been
taught that much of one's sense of identity was merely a
construct, made up of a complex overlay of thoughts and
feelings derived from experiences and interpretations or
misinterpretations of those experiences - in other words,
a self-created story. She remembered one of her teachers
describing the personality as merely a mask worn by the
True Self.

"OK, so I'm not my sense of identity. My True Self -
whatever that is - extends beyond that. Part of my work
- should I become an Initiate - will be to reconnect with

that True Self. Well, not quite reconnect," she corrected herself, "since there was never any disconnection. It's more a matter of working through the misconceptions and misinterpretations that keep me from seeing what is, and from remembering who I really am."

It was all so confusing. Sometimes it seemed that the teachings contradicted themselves. Her personality was only a mask, yet she was supposed to find out what she - did they mean her mask? - wanted. Personality or "self" was but an inconsequential, incomplete expression of one's soul. What then, was the purpose of finding answers about her individual wants and needs? What did they want from her, why did they send her home, and what was she supposed to accomplish now that she was here? The only thing she felt certain about was that today was not the day she would find the answers. Later she would be meeting David and some other friends for lunch. She put aside her questions and prepared for a day of fun and socializing. At least that was her original plan…

Chapter Ten

AS SHE SAT in the restaurant with her friends, Naomi became increasingly uncomfortable. "Stop beating around the bush, Searra, and just come out and say what you mean. Are you implying that you think I'm a coward who is avoiding life's challenges by wanting to enter the Temple? It won't be the first time I've heard that accusation."

Searra turned bright red and averted her eyes. "I have no idea what you're talking about, Naomi. I think you're just being overly sensitive. Maybe it has something to do with your being sent home. Really, Naomi. If that's what you're worrying about, don't. None of us are judging you as a failure."

Naomi felt the distinct sensation of having just been

socked in the stomach. She could almost feel the breath being knocked out of her, along with feelings of pain and discomfort in her abdomen. If it weren't for her time in the Temple she would have thought she was being absurd. Clearly, no one had struck her physically, but just as clearly, Searra had struck a blow with the intention of causing Naomi pain, embarrassment and discomfort. She felt her own anger rise in response when, without warning, her inner vision opened and the scene took on a very different appearance. Strange that after so many months of working to open this vision, without success, it should open spontaneously in the middle of a restaurant while lunching with her friends. Caught off guard, the immensity and beauty of what she was seeing completely swept her into an altered state of consciousness.

Time was fluid and non-linear. Depending on where she focused, she could see either "past," "present," or "future." She looked "back" to the moment before the awakening. Searra at that moment was a jumble of conflicting emotions - anger, jealousy, and longing were the strongest. Each emotion created a swirling pattern of Energy associated with images that floated around it. These images represented significant moments in Searra's life in which she had made decisions that locked her into particular patterns of behavior. By focusing attention on any of these images, they could be "read" like detailed and illustrated storybooks. Naomi saw how people's personal decisions had the power to limit the free flowing of Energy and keep them from uniting with their True Self. She realized that this was how the mask of personality came to be. Behind the mask was a pure and vast field of light, filled with love and compassion - vast, expansive, and connected to the Infinite.

Naomi could now clearly see that the self existing in the here and now was indeed just a tiny aspect of a greater whole. It was humbling to realize that her personality was nothing more than a rigid conglomeration of previous decisions and misconceptions that kept her from being one with and living deeply from her spiritual essence. So this was what the Temple had been trying to teach her. Only by facing and working through these erroneous assumptions could she learn to live life from an increasingly soulful perspective. If she could release her false beliefs, she would expand past her limited perceptions into the Infinite, realizing unity with the All. The concept was exhilarating and so terrifyingly overwhelming that it frightened her *back into normal waking consciousness; and she promptly passed out...*

There was a sound - a voice. Yes, that's what it was, a voice. Speaking.

Speaking? What is speaking? thought the part of her that felt fuzzy and disoriented.

Oh, yes, a form of communication between two separate entities. The other part remembered.

Separate? What does it mean - this thing called separate?

She became aware of the external voice again.

She? This entity has a name? No, not a name - a label - something to differentiate it from the one speaking. The confusion was starting to clear.

"Naomi, are you OK?" David asked once again.

Naomi - that had a familiar feel to it. Another label? No, this one was a name - her name.

"Naomi? Can you hear me? NAOMI!"

She rubbed her forehead and then her eyes. Gazing around, she wondered how she came to be on the restaurant veranda, with David standing over her looking worried. "David?" She watched his face shift and change.

"Brian? David, how can you also be Brian?"

"No, Naomi, I'm David. You're safe here. I have called for a Temple Healer. Someone will be here soon. You…I don't know exactly what happened. All of a sudden you became very still. You had this odd look on your face and…well, then you fainted. So, I brought you here and asked that someone call for a healer. Do you remember any of what happened? Are you OK? Do you know who I am?"

"Of course I know who you are. So much more than just David." She reached out her hand and tenderly touched David's face. "Really, I'm OK. It all just opened up without warning."

"What opened up? What are you talking about?" David looked worried.

"The vision, of course." Her eyes still had a faraway look to them. "There are so very many dimensions. Such a beautiful kaleidoscope of interconnections. It makes perfect sense now. There is no past or future - it is all in the now."

She paused and gazed intently at his face before continuing. "I'm married to you when you are Brian. We're both doctors and have a beautiful life together, but you can't deal with the spiritual dimensions. I'm not too comfortable with them myself - though I get quite an unexpected education about them. I learn to refrain from talking to you about them. In that time/space, they change my life, but still I shy away from exploring them further. I fear it will create distance between us. In this dimension, here and now, you are unfailingly respectful of my desire to explore them - refusing to stand in my way. Perfect balance, see?"

She frowned and bit her lower lip. "But not all of the other selves are nice in the other dimensions." Her voice became a soft murmur. "So many other dimensions... all of them me, and yet not me. How can we be in so many different times and places? All so different, yet entwined..." Her eyes widened and her voice became agitated. "When I am him, I'm so angry! The world is violent and nobody cares about me - or anybody else. I do terrible things to people. When you are Joey, I kill your father." She looked him in the eye. "I'm so sorry, Joey. You were just a little boy and you worshipped him and then I killed him. I'm sorry. I didn't know you were there or that you saw the whole thing. So sorry..." A look of confusion crossed her face. "He's your father, so

how can he also be my father? Oh, of course - different
dimensions. He is your father when you are Joey, but
my father - Jonathan Sarton - when I am Naomi. Don't
you see? That's why I can't hurt him again. When he
was your father, he was such a good man, and I killed
him. But it's really so beautiful when you see from the
soul perspective where we are all interconnected. In that
dimension," the otherworldly look in her eyes deepened,
"I kill him, yet he saves me. In that dimension, I can't
stop thinking about him. Part of me thinks he's a stupid
jerk for getting involved, but I also can't stop thinking
about the fact that he does get involved. I mean, he
doesn't even know the girl, but risks his life to save her.
So I start to think that maybe good people do exist, and
that gives me hope. Suddenly, I'm not so proud of myself
and what I have done. I start to wonder if maybe I could
be a better person. I can't keep hurting people. I find
a young kid, like myself - been beaten up pretty badly
by the world. I can make him one of the gang - he's got
the killer instinct. But something's different now. I take
him under my wing. I help him and then he helps a lot
of other kids. See what I mean? It's all perfect. We have
to grow toward the Light. We have to experience it all

in order to do so. These experiences are just different aspects of our being - kind of like dream states - until we become attached to them. That's when we lose our clarity and no longer recognize our connection to the Infinite. You see, it's not about good or bad or tragic or happy. It's about balance - the perfect balance of opposites. When we achieve perfect balance, we find our perfect center and we expand to become One. It's about acceptance, and harmony and love. That's all there is to it. So easy. Just so easy and..." Her voice had become progressively softer and her words more garbled as she slipped into what looked like a peaceful sleep.

David just sat there and shook his head. He wasn't sure that anything she had just said made sense. But then again, perhaps it did.

The Temple sent three healers. They spent about ten minutes alone with her, and then told David she would be fine and not to worry. They left refusing to answer any questions or say anything more.

Now that Naomi was awake, alert, and feeling better, she just wanted to return home. As she reentered the restaurant dining room to say good-bye, she realized that her perception had not completely returned to its usual state. Looking at her friends, she became aware of things she had been blissfully unconscious of previously. She was learning how complex human interactions really were.

She could see so much more - it was overwhelming. She now understood why Searra had been unkind to her. Searra was attracted to David. Her Energy reached out to him with longing, and to Naomi with resentment for being the focus of David's affection. David was completely unaware of her attraction, but also kept his distance from her for reasons he never questioned. Naomi doubted that Searra had ever admitted to these feelings - even to herself. To Naomi, this Energy was sharp and uncomfortable to be around.

To further complicate the scene, Samuel, another of their mutual friends, was attracted to Naomi. Unlike Searra, he accepted his feelings and consciously dealt with them. Therefore, he was not left with unconscious anger and resentment. Outwardly, he expressed only his deep respect for Naomi. He nursed his disappointment quietly, while suppressing any inappropriate feelings. The Energy was not uncomfortable, though he radiated disappointment and sadness.

Naomi wondered if any human interaction was what

it appeared to be on the surface. As soon as Searra had made her attacking comments, Naomi's friend Bonnie had risen to her defense. At the time, she had assumed that Bonnie's motive had been loyalty and an instinct to protect a friend. That had been part of it, but it was not that simple. Now she could see that Bonnie always carried anger and resentment below the surface of her awareness. Bonnie's fury at Searra's insensitive and provocative comments was displaced anger, layered with complexity. It was a strong Energy and showered down upon the group. Without anyone understanding or being aware of what was happening or why it was happening, Bonnie's anger had stirred up agitation in almost everyone. In her current state of consciousness, Naomi could "see" that Bonnie's mother had wounded her repeatedly throughout her life with her sharp tongue and rageful disposition. It was for this reason that she had been so sensitive and reactive to Searra's verbal jabs.

Naomi was surrounded by jumbled images, impressions and swirling Energies. At this particular moment the Energies were not pleasant, and the discord was painful to her newly awakened perceptions. She felt physically assaulted by Searra's anger and jealousy,

Samuel's denied longings, Bonnie's displaced rage, and everyone else's discomfort and confusion. She watched the play of Energies and how they mingled and grew - each person's negativity arousing and opening further negative feelings in everyone around them. The sensations swirled with such intensity that she wanted to scream, and was afraid she might faint once again.

I can't take this! she thought. *Can't they see what they're doing? If even one of them would calm down, it would help stop the cascading effects of the negative Energies. Just look at Bonnie. I know she's angry, but the strength of her anger comes from her personal wounds from the past.* She projected her thoughts toward Bonnie. *Can't you feel that you're also doing this out of love and loyalty to me in the present? Searra can't help herself, but you can. Feel compassion for her. Forgive your own mother. Trust in me that I will be fine and can take care of myself. Feel your connection to the love that surrounds and permeates us.* She gazed lovingly at Bonnie and sensed the beauty that was part of Bonnie as it is part of us all. As she continued to gaze, she saw the swirling Energies surrounding Bonnie calm. She realized with surprise, that she was the cause of the Energy shift.

Her own Energies were interacting with and soothing Bonnie's. Not knowing exactly how all this worked, she set the intention of soothing and harmonizing the discord within the Energies of the group. As she did so, she felt herself growing calmer, more centered, and more connected to the Infinite. Gradually, the feelings of being assaulted by negativity retreated, and she watched her friends reach out to each other and begin to work together in greater harmony. She had effected this change. For the second time that day, she felt both elated and terrified. Deeply exhausted, she was ready to go home.

She was awed by what had happened, and was continuing to happen. In every interaction she could now see the interplay of the Subtle Energies. Nothing was just what it appeared to be. Always, the unseen Energies were as powerful and important as the words and gestures people used - and in some ways more so - since they affected people emotionally and at the core of their being, without their conscious awareness.

She was having one of the most amazing experiences of her life and yet was unable to share it with anyone around her. It made her feel different, as though she didn't belong. It made her feel lonely. It made her long for Temple life in a way she never had before. She now understood why she had been sent home. Finally she knew with certainty that she was ready to leave her old life behind and dedicate herself to the life of an Initiate.

She spent one last week at home with her father before returning to the Temple. She had no idea what would happen next. If they sent her far away from her District, she didn't know if or when she might see her father again. When she told him of her awakening and of her decision, he took the news well. Though she could see that his heart was still heavy, it was also more open. He was healing, and in that healing he was able to release her. With her new insights she understood why she had always been so afraid of hurting him. Now she could leave without guilt. This enabled her to focus on moving forward, rather than on what she would be leaving behind.

Chapter Eleven

AS SHE ENTERED the Temple, she understood why people believed it was built on hallowed ground. It was not the ground that was sacred; rather, it was the Energies generated by the Initiates that created the sacred feeling. Unlike her experiences at home with her friends, here everyone's Energy flowed and interacted harmoniously. Everyone was doing exactly what he or she was meant to do and enjoyed doing. Mother Danielle, the Temple administrator, was organized and efficient. It gave her a deep sense of satisfaction to keep things running smoothly. Brother Joseph worked in the garden. His greatest love was to tend growing things and to watch them flourish under his touch. Brother Samuels liked nothing better than to talk to people and help them out.

His task was to greet the many visitors who came to the Temple each day. Naomi felt the peaceful contentment generated by people who were doing what they were suited for. It generated a wondrously deep feeling of serenity within her. She smiled inwardly, confident that whatever task the Temple chose for her would be perfect.

She headed to the far side of the Temple grounds, where those seeking Initiation were housed. There she would meet Brother Francis, who was in charge of the students. With a bounce in her step and a broad smile on her face, she walked through the garden. Suddenly, she became aware of a discordance in the Energy. It felt like an electric jolt, disrupting the peaceful flow. Without thinking, she turned toward the garden to her left and hurried down the path. When she reached the fruit orchard, she saw Sister Jeanine cradling her left hand. Already two healers were at her side, stemming the flow of blood where she had cut her hand while pruning. Father Jerome, who was watching over it all, nodded to Naomi and walked over to her.

"Glad to see you here." He looked at her with his piercing gaze. "But then I rarely make mistakes." His face broke into a smile which did little to shed light on his cryptic comment. "I believe Brother Francis is expecting you." He turned around and returned to Sister Jeanine, whose wound had been tended and who was now laughing and joking with the healers. The Energy was restored to its earlier serenity.

Naomi continued to the student residence and Training Hall for non-Initiates. Upon entering, she was greeted by a wave of chaotic, undisciplined Energy so unlike the peaceful flow in the rest of the Temple. She grinned as she realized why the new recruits were kept so far from the rest of the Temple. The grin faded as she began to experience feelings of irritability brought about by the jarring dissonance of wildly unruly Energies. *Well, I suppose I will not be sent to train new recruits, she thought. Recently I was one of them, and now I can barely tolerate being around them.* A moment of apprehension followed that thought as she worried that her heightened awareness might render her too sensitive to function comfortably in many situations. Immediately she dismissed the thought, reassuring herself that they would find an appropriate task to fit her temperament.

Brother Francis was delayed, so Naomi spent the afternoon with the new candidates. Their training, designed to awaken them spiritually, included having to confront many painful truths that kept them "asleep" - especially misconceptions about themselves and their narrow view of the world around them. Their "awakenings" were the cause of the chaotic Energies Naomi was experiencing.

She was surprised to feel subtle tensions and conflicts between the individual candidates. Things were clearly not flowing as smoothly here as in the rest of the Temple. Sensing a sudden pleasant shift within the Energies, she observed petty squabbles and tensions easing. Brother Francis had returned. With a feeling of awe she realized that his presence modulated the chaos. She remembered how she too had used Energy to help restore tranquility among her friends after Searra and Bonnie's discordant exchange. She marveled at the power of Energies to affect not only individuals, but entire groups. If Brother Francis, by himself, could affect the flow of the entire Candidates Hall, she could only imagine how a group of Initiates could help keep peace in society at large. The implications were mind-boggling.

Putting these thoughts aside, she rose to meet Brother Francis. They would discuss her upcoming Initiation

Ceremony and, hopefully, her place within the Temple.

Two hours later, Naomi was both intrigued and frustrated. While her conversation with Brother Francis had been fascinating, he had revealed nothing of her future destiny. The candidates she had trained with had already been Initiated. Since Initiation was always done as a group, she had assumed she would have to wait several months for the new candidates to be ready. This, however, would not be the case. She would be Initiated the following week, and she would be Initiated by herself. This was most unusual.

While waiting for Initiation, she spent a great deal of her time with Father Jerome. While he also revealed nothing to her about her future, they talked about the Temple and discussed her insights into the subtle workings of Energies. The night before her Initiation found her restless and barely able to sleep.

Chapter Twelve

NAOMI AWOKE before the crack of dawn and made her way to the Temple's Inner Sanctum at the foot of Craigshorn Mountain, overlooking Nanchon Province. No non-Initiate had even been there, and most Initiates had been there only once - the day of their Initiation. As she approached the gates to the Sanctum, she was greeted by three women she had never before seen. They were dressed in graceful white garments that fell in long, soft folds to their feet. Silently, they beckoned her to follow. As the gates began to open, she got her first glimpse of what lay beyond. As far as her eyes could see were beautiful gardens, laced with inviting paths and tall lush trees. She had never seen such beauty or felt such peace. Transfixed, she began to cry with both joy and sorrow - joy to know such a feeling of completeness, and sorrow that she would ever have to leave. The eldest of the three women gently tapped her on her shoulder. She looked at this woman, who was clearly the leader among the three women. Naomi assumed she must be some sort of Healer, for she emanated strength, peace, and an astonishing depth of love, leaving Naomi feeling embraced and healed in places she didn't even know were wounded. She found herself once again weeping. She had no idea how much time had passed, nor did it seem to matter. When the tears stopped, the women calmly walked on, and she followed them up a beautifully cultivated path. They came upon a fork in the trail. To the right was a broad, tree-lined path. To the left was a narrow trail lined with beautiful flowers. The women turned left and Naomi followed, her senses stirred by the lush beauty and intoxicating smells of the profuse and beautiful blooms. They stopped. There, surrounded by exotic plants, was a small, crystal-clear, round pool. Its water began at the mountaintop and flowed down a steep rock wall to fill the pool, before gently cascading down small boulders leading to a larger lake.

For the first time, the older woman spoke. "Here

you will be purified in the sacred waters before your Initiation. As you bathe in these waters, your soul will be cleansed. Not all come here before their Initiation, but you have your own unique path. You are a Child of Spirit. You have heard this before but do not yet remember. You have your own path. You are meant to be a healer of mankind. Long have you labored, many are the painful experiences, and many are the joys you have met along the way. Always your journey has been leading here. You are not yet complete. There is still more to do. But you have come far enough to be able to bathe in the sacred waters. When you are finished, you may don this robe. It is like ours except that the trim is of a purple hue. We will wait here until you are done. Enter the waters. Have no concern for time - the water will tell you when to leave." She placed a towel and the robe upon a boulder, then turned and left.

Naomi dipped her hand in the water, expecting it to be icy cold. To her surprise it was refreshingly cool, but not cold. Reassured, she disrobed and slowly immersed herself in the waters. Not knowing what to expect, she tried to quiet her thoughts and open herself to the experience. Slowly, a feeling of peaceful emptiness consumed her, and her sense of "herself" began to fade. She was one with the water and the trees and the flowers and the sky, and finally with the universe. No longer were there boundaries between self and not-self, for everything was interconnected. All was One. Images began to form and stories began to unfold. A consciousness - that at certain times and places was called Naomi - observed. Deeply stirring stories of joy and sorrow, of struggles and disappointments, of triumphs and failures followed one after the other. A native boy was being abducted by slave traders; an angry young man was killing another man who was trying to save an innocent young girl; a young tribeswoman was terrified as she was thrown into a dark locked room; a physician was learning to open her heart; and so they continued, one after the other. The stories slowed down and new experiences took their place. There was a sense of other people, a feeling of familiarity and comfort and of belonging. Merging… separate identities fading… the power building…bliss…the return of a familiar terror… and once again she was Naomi. She longed to go back to what she had glimpsed, and just as strongly feared to go back. Once again, tears streamed down her face. She had no idea when they had started or why they were there. The water started to feel cold, and with utter certainty she knew that the time had come for her to climb out. Without further thought, she dried herself off and donned the white robe. The ground beckoned to her and she sat quietly, feeling empty and peaceful as she awaited the return of her guides.

The wait was not long. When the women returned, Naomi was aware of a penetrating scrutiny emanating from the eldest of the three. It was not intrusive, and left her feeling safe and warm. Though she felt drawn to this quiet woman, the feelings were easily pushed aside, replaced once again with quiet and peaceful emptiness. Her guides beckoned and she followed them back the way they had come - this time turning down the larger tree-lined path. The path widened, trees thinned, and there before them stood a beautiful white domed building. The building was round with what could be considered four "corners," since equally spaced around the sides of the buildings were four enormous rounded spires, each with a large arched entry door. She could see that one door was open, and it was to this one that her guides led her. The three stepped aside, motioned for her to enter, and then followed her inside.

She had not realized from the outside that the domed ceiling was made of a translucent substance allowing the entire interior of the building to be filled with warm, glowing, natural light. The effect was breathtaking, and mesmerizing. In a trancelike state, she walked to the center of the room and, without conscious thought, sat directly on top of a brightly colored mosaic pattern in the tile floor. She was herself and not herself - aware of the personality and feelings of the entity called Naomi and simultaneously aware of so much more. A man entered through one of the other doors. She knew him, but not as he was now. At one time he had worn the name Gandji, and at another time the name Douglas Fairway. She felt warmth and trust for this being, and also love. For a moment this reaction confused her, for what could one feel for any living entity other than love? Another presence entered - she knew that the one called Naomi referred to this one as Father Jerome. Still others entered - each one familiar in some way. Finally there was a feeling of wholeness in the room, and with it an understanding that all who were meant to be there were now present. Energies swirled among the entities in the room, and though no words were spoken, much communication took place.

Expanded awareness… blissful wholeness… understandings beyond words and concepts… unconditional Love… all within Oneness. Then a return to a sense of smallness, individual consciousness, and a diminution back to Naomi - feeling separate and alone. It was complete. Slowly and silently the others took their leave. Only Father Jerome remained.

Quietly he sat down next to her. Words were still hard for Naomi to form, but then she had the sense that they were unnecessary. She was an Initiate. She was now Sister Naomi. Tomorrow she might be full of questions. Now, she just wanted to rest. She looked at Father Jerome.

"It's OK, child. We will talk tomorrow. Would you like me to show you to a room where you can sleep?"

Gratefully, Sister Naomi nodded. Soon she found herself in a warm, soft bed, blissfully sliding into the Dreamworld.

—⟋⟍—

She had been here before. The orbs floated in space, interconnecting, trying to form a pattern. Power just below the surface - but some imbalance was keeping the design from forming. The light grew and the boundaries began to dissolve, but one point of darkness radiated strongly. Uncertainty... fear...need for control...clinging to "I-ness"... and then it was gone, all dissolved. She reached out to...What is it that she was reaching for? She felt desolate and alone...

—⟋⟍—

Naomi awoke feeling rested but strangely empty. This was not how she expected to feel the day after her blissful Initiation. Yesterday was a haze of mysterious events that in retrospect made little sense and shed little light on what her future would hold. Once again, she felt a sensation of being both herself yet not quite herself. The "thinking" rational part of her wanted answers and direction, wondering what she was supposed to do and where she was supposed to be. Somehow she realized that such needs belonged to her old world and had little relevance now. When she stopped thinking and questioning, she was rewarded with feelings of peace. Focusing on the immediate moment, she became aware of her physical needs and of being ravenously hungry. She took a moment to look around the simple quarters she had slept in. On the chair near the bed was the robe she had worn the day before. Having no other clothes to choose from, she donned the robe and left the room to explore what lay beyond. The room's only door led into a quiet hallway that looked the same in both directions. Calmly she turned to the right and began walking. It didn't take her long to find the dining hall.

Father Jerome looked up as she entered and gestured for her to join him. He sat with the three women who had been her guides the day before. Looking around the room, she recognized some of the people who had been present at her Initiation. Yesterday they had been quiet, contemplative, and serious. The atmosphere today was very different. The room was full of light-hearted banter, camaraderie, and laughter. Feeling a bit shy and awkward, she made her way to the table and took a seat. The center of the table was piled high with food. While her mouth watered and her stomach growled, she felt hesitant and unsure of herself. Should she wait to be asked or just reach for the food? She looked around the room, trying to see what the proper behavior would be. As she hesitantly prepared to reach for the sumptuous feast before her, Father Jerome reassured her.

"I'm sure you must be quite hungry. Please help yourself. As you can see, food is plentiful."

She looked at him gratefully and began filling her plate. Before she could begin her meal, her attention was drawn away by the melodious voice of yesterday's elder guide. She didn't even know this woman's name, but was comforted and warmed by her powerful and healing presence. She listened contentedly to her voice.

"What you experienced yesterday will leave you feeling a little strange today and also very hungry. Those are normal responses. There will be food available here all day. Don't hesitate to indulge yourself in more than three good meals today." She gazed at Naomi with a look that seemed to penetrate down to Naomi's core. With someone else it might have felt intrusive, but Naomi didn't mind a bit. In fact, it felt reassuring and seemed to complete an emptiness Naomi had not even been consciously aware of.

She met the woman's gaze and once again felt shy and awkward. "Thank you" was all she managed to say.

"You are most welcome. Well, I must leave now. I am sure we will see each other again." The woman smiled at her as she rose gracefully and left the room.

"Father Jerome, who is she?"

"Ah, full of curiosity, aren't you?" Father Jerome laughed. "Today is not the day for questions or answers. Take some time for yourself. Initiation changes a person right down to their cells. It can be rather disorienting. You may notice subtle - or not so subtle - changes in your thought patterns, emotional responses, and even your perceptions. Today, just relax. Tomorrow we will talk."

Chapter Thirteen

THIS TIME THE ORBS morphed into new shapes - growing arms and legs and becoming vaguely humanoid. One opened its mouth as if to speak, then opened it wider. She fled in terror. She didn't want it to eat her and consume her - digesting her very essence into its core. The others looked on sadly, beckoning to her, trying to entice her into their cannibalistic ritual.

"NO!" she screamed. "I am Naomi Sarton. I exist. I am! Go away and stop tormenting me."

They backed away and the terror subsided. She sobbed and felt bereft. Why was she not relieved?

Her father and David reached out to her and she felt their concern. She reached back and their hands connected. The reassurance was short-lived, followed by rage and frustration. She could only touch them on the surface. It wasn't enough! Couldn't they feel how superficial it was? So much was missing. She ran from them into a dense forest. The forest creatures squawked and bellowed, and she filled her mind with their incoherent chatter. A fog enveloped her, emanating from the top of her own head. It was comforting, wrapping her in a sweet blanket of ignorant bliss. She snuggled into it.

—⁂—

On the second day after her Initiation, Sister Naomi awoke feeling more refreshed and alert. Quickly she jotted down her strange dream, donned her robe and left the room, looking forward to her meeting with Father Jerome. She met him in the dining hall and after breakfast they walked to the flower gardens to talk.

Father Jerome asked a lot of questions and listened attentively as she told him about her experiences and her dreams. They talked for a long time, yet Naomi was no closer to knowing her future. She listened hopefully as Father Jerome continued to speak.

"You have been through some very interesting experiences recently. Tell me how it has changed you and your sense of the world."

Naomi sat quietly. So much had happened that had completely altered her worldview. Underlying all these changes was her newfound awareness of the power of unseen Energies to affect and alter both people and circumstances. She had become aware of a phenomenon few people even believed existed, yet she suspected it was one of the most powerful forces in the universe. By itself, it was a force that was neither good nor evil. Whether it was used for destruction or healing was entirely up to the person or persons wielding it. Yes, person or "persons"... She returned to her memory of the impact she had had on her friends when she used the Energy to calm the group, and of the ability of Brother Francis to affect the students in the Training Hall, and once again wondered about the power that could be utilized by "persons" wielding the Energies together. She tried putting her thoughts into words.

"Before, I was ignorant, but now I know the power that one individual can have on his or her surroundings. I have become aware of the impact of our thoughts and feelings on others. I have seen that what we project from our mind and our emotions can have a greater effect than what we say with our mouths. Sadly, most people are completely unaware of what is being projected from their minds and from their emotions, and therefore fail to take responsibility for its effects. I have come to understand that the heart is much more powerful than the head."

Father Jerome responded, "Properly understood, all of what you have spoken about can be turned into a tool for healing. Would you like to learn more about all of this?"

"Yes," Naomi responded without hesitation.

"Then you shall," Father Jerome said with a smile. "You will become a student of these Energies by learning to use them to heal others. For now, you will work with Sister Sandrina as her apprentice. You may continue to live in this part of the Temple and you will remain in your current room. You will be given one other set of robes and may bring in a few personal belongings, but for now you will keep your life simple and uncluttered."

"You keep saying 'for now.' Where will I go from here?" Naomi asked.

"You will go where you are meant to go, and you will go when the time is ripe. It will all fall into place without any of us doing anything to make it so and without any of us knowing the exact details," Father Jerome said gently.

"Consider this as part of keeping your life simple. At present there is no need to know anything more. Trust <u>this</u> moment; be whole in <u>this</u> moment; be healed in <u>this</u> moment and you set the groundwork for being whole and healed and living in trust in every moment. Have faith, child. You will fulfill your destiny. It has been a long time coming, but you need not wait much longer. Go now. Tomorrow morning you begin your work with Sister Sandrina." Clearly, the meeting was at an end and no more would be said. Naomi returned to her room, wondering once again what her future would hold.

Chapter Fourteen

SISTER SANDRINA was a tall elegant woman, who emanated both power and tranquility. Naomi liked her instantly. She was a mediator who helped people work out their conflicts in a fascinating and unique way.

On the seventh day of Naomi's training, Sister Sandrina had explained all that she could: "There is only so much I can teach you, Sister Naomi. The rest you must learn through experience. Today you will observe and then share your perceptions. I am sure you will find this quite interesting. Come with me. I am meeting with two farmers who are having a difficult time with each other."

For the first time since her Initiation, Naomi left the Inner Sanctum. She accompanied Sandrina to the

Hall of Resolution, where people came to air their grievances. She was instructed to sit quietly and observe the proceedings.

—⚒—

"That land is mine, Benton! Your land stops at the big oak tree and that last acre is mine. You are growing your crops on my land and I won't have it. I need that extra land to feed my family."

"And you, Jensen, are a crazy, selfish old fool. You know full well that my father and his father before him have always cultivated that piece of land. When we were still little boys and my father broke his leg, you and your father came over and helped us harvest the crops from that same piece of land. Don't you remember? You helped us gather 'our' crops. There was no talk of it being your land. You can't just go change the rules after three generations. And what of my family? We barely make it as it is and certainly use everything we grow there. We would go hungry without it."

"My grandfather didn't give your family the land. He had only one daughter, and your family had three sons so he let your grandfather cultivate the land since he didn't have enough hands to work that land and had fewer mouths to feed. It was a generous favor - not a lifetime gift. Times have changed and now I need that land and I want it back."

"We don't know what our grandfathers said and why they did what they did. All I know is that since my earliest memories we have grown our crops there, and before now there has never been talk about not having the right to do so."

"That's a lie! You know full well that we had that land before your grandfather started using it."

"Yes, I know that. But how do you know that the land wasn't originally ours, and that generations before that, my ancestors allowed your ancestors use of it? The land is mine and it will stay that way. You have no right to kick me off it. Even as a child you always wanted what you wanted, without regard for anyone else. You haven't changed a bit."

"I haven't changed? And what about you? Do you want me to remind you of what you were like as a child? Do you think I have forgotten how you mistreated my brother and…"

"Gentlemen," Sandrina chose this moment to step

in. "Obviously, you have had this discussion before and it is getting you nowhere. I have heard what each of you thinks. Let's take a break. We will meet back here in two hours." She turned and gestured to Naomi to follow her as she left the room.

"What did you see?" Sandrina asked Naomi.

"Clearly, they are very upset with each other, and neither of them is willing to compromise."

"Yes, that is true. But go deeper. Tell me what you see in each of their Energies."

At first Naomi felt uncertain. She had never before consciously tried to explore the Energies in that way. She closed her eyes and focused on the two men. Images and feelings that were not her own began to flood her awareness. The more she relaxed and surrendered, the stronger the feelings became. It was somewhat disorienting and a bit overwhelming to experience feelings in her own body and psyche that were not her own. It made her feel angry and intruded upon, leading to feelings of impatient agitation. Why had Father Jerome sent her here? Clearly, she would not make a good mediator, especially since she could so easily imagine going back into that room and yelling at these two men for their small-mindedness. She felt inadequate, at least until she realized that both the anger and the negative feelings were not her own. Focusing on these two farmers had caused her own psyche to shift. Here was yet another indication of how powerful people's thoughts and feelings were. With greater confidence, she reached back into their Energy fields, amazed and delighted at how much information she could sense. Naomi opened her eyes and began to share her perceptions with Sister Sandrina.

"Both are blinded by rage. Jensen, the one who wants the land back, feels..." Naomi searched for the right word "...insufficient... inadequate." She closed her eyes as images began to form. "When he was a boy there was a problem with his mother. Sickness, perhaps? It feels like she was unable to properly care for him for...maybe for as long as several years. I see his father trying hard to be there for him but having little extra time or energy. His older brother took on a much greater share of work and responsibility since their mother was incapacitated. Jensen tried to help, but was too young to be of much assistance. His brother teased him mercilessly - in reality because he was jealous and thought Jensen had it easy. The brother resented that he had to work so hard and

take care of Jensen as well. All this, unfortunately, left
Jensen feeling inadequate on the one hand because
he wasn't much help, and at the same time angry and
deprived because no one had the time to attend to him.
Now he constantly feels that he never gets enough. He
also feels that no matter how hard he works, he is never
good enough and never appreciated. Times are hard now,
increasing his feelings of failure because food is scarce,
yet he also feels deprived and wants to angrily blame
others to cover over his feelings of shame. Right now he
is blaming Benton."

She switched her focus to Benton. "Benton, at the
best of times, can be a generous and good-hearted man.
He and Jensen grew up together and were very close." She
could see an image of the two young boys playing and
laughing and being inseparable. Suddenly she saw a tall,
dark energy shadowing their play. As the image came
into focus, she saw Jensen's older brother, manipulating
Benton into giving him his toys as well as bullying him
into giving him a tool that belonged to Benton's father.
Benton then lied to his father to cover up the fact that
the tool was missing. Benton never forgave Jensen's
brother, and years later expended a great deal of energy

in pulling nasty pranks in order to get even. The need for revenge originated in his continuing guilt over lying to his father and taking his tool. Naomi was amazed that could see this so clearly. But she couldn't figure out how this was relevant to what was going on now between him and Jensen. As soon as she formed this as a question, she began feeling the answer. She explained her insights to Sister Sandrina. "Part of the difficulty for Benton in resolving the current dilemma stems from an incident many years ago between Benton and Jensen's brother. The experience has left Benton with so much anger and guilt that he is unwilling to give Jensen's family anything - especially if it involves taking away from his own family."

"Very good, Sister Naomi," Sister Sandrina said approvingly. "Now go deeper into the subtleties and tell me about each man's Energy field."

Once again Naomi sat quietly and closed her eyes. She focused first on Jensen. She was immediately aware of feeling tight angry resistance, stubborn inflexibility and feelings of deprivation, as well as a sense of desperate hunger. The sensations reached for her as if trying to invade her and take everything she had. Her instinctive reaction was to hold on to and hoard whatever she could.

Seeing what Jensen's Energy projected, she understood Benton's refusal to compromise. She switched her awareness to Benton and felt his fear and distrust. Fearing that someone might force him against his will, he shut down the minute he felt anyone trying to push him in any direction. His irrational refusal was frustrating, and incited her to want to fight him and become demanding. No wonder he and Jensen were unwilling to compromise with each other!

Clearly, their inability to resolve their conflict had little to do with what they were fighting about. Their words were about acreage and details of ownership, but the conflict resided in their feelings and distrust caused by past traumas. Their fight was not about land, but about their personal fears. Lost in feelings of victimization, they kept behaving in ways that ensured they became victims.

"Sandrina, I can see the problem from an Energetic perspective; the question is how to use this knowledge to reach a solution. Getting them to work together seems like a long, arduous task, requiring each of them to see their own mistaken assumptions and then heal their wounds and resistance. This could take months, yet I've seen you resolve even more difficult conflicts in a very short time. What's the use of what I have seen if I'm no closer to being able to help?"

"Naomi, what could you change in them energetically in order to help them reach a resolution?"

Once again Naomi closed her eyes and reached within. "They have these thick walls that keep their Energies and therefore their thoughts trapped and stagnant. This creates rigidity - both mentally and emotionally. Each time one of them encounters the other's resistance, it causes his own resistance to grow exponentially; so the more they fight, the more they become rigidly locked in combat. If there were some way to unblock these Energies, I believe they would have an easier time finding a solution."

"You are correct, Sister Naomi. So go ahead and unblock their Energies."

"How?" Naomi looked startled. "How in the world am I supposed to just unblock their Energies?"

Sandrina looked at her calmly with a hint of a smile. "Try," was all she said.

So, Naomi tried. As she closed her eyes, focusing inwardly on the two men, she began to feel their resistance as if it were in her own body. Entering into a meditative state, she monitored and soothed the uncomfortable sensations. Gradually, as she accessed a deeper state of meditation, she became less conscious of her surroundings. When awareness returned to the immediate present, she felt more peaceful. "I'm not sure what I did, but I can feel less resistance now - less, but not none."

"A good start, Sister Naomi. Soon it will be time to meet with them again. Then we will see what we will see." Without further explanation, she rose and left the room.

When Naomi reentered the Hall of Resolution, Jensen and Benton were already there. Immediately she could sense the difference in the air. There was a companionable ease in the way they were relating to each other that had not been present before. However, she still sensed tensions right below the surface that could be triggered easily. This session was less fraught with hostility, but still they could not reach a resolution. Disappointed that the problem was still unresolved, she voiced her frustrations to Sandrina.

"You're way too hard on yourself, Sister Naomi. Unblocking someone's Energy field has a profoundly powerful ripple effect and is potentially dangerous. What you accomplished was nothing short of amazing - enough so that I would have stopped you if you had taken it any further." Seeing Naomi's look of confusion, she continued. "We all affect each other's Energy fields. We do so every time we interact with or even think about somebody. Some people can do so more than others, and a few - like you - can be trained to do so very effectively."

"Then why would you have stopped me if I could have accomplished more? Aren't we trying to get them past their blocks and resistance so they can resolve their conflict?"

"Do you have any idea what happens when someone's Energy is rapidly unblocked?" Sandrina focused her gaze on Naomi.

"They feel better and have clearer perceptions?" Naomi asked hesitantly.

"Yes, well at least eventually. But that would not be their first experience." Sandrina sighed. "I hope I am making the right decision here. Father Jerome asked me to teach and train you, yet has given me very little time." She sighed again. Walking toward Naomi, she asked permission to place her hands on Naomi's head.

As soon as she did so, Naomi felt a tingling, followed by a sensation of heat throughout her body. She began to shake, then broke into tears of utter desolation and abandonment. Her childhood had been full of love and nurturing, but suddenly all she could feel was the loneliness of growing up without her mother. The pain was overwhelming. She doubled over, clenching her arms across her chest, and wept uncontrollably.

"Yes, it is quite painful, and you have always protected yourself from feeling this, but by doing so, you also kept yourself from ever truly opening to love." Sandrina put her arms around Naomi and held her as Naomi continued to weep.

Finally Naomi was able to speak. "OK. You made your point," she said shakily. "If I had done more with Jensen and Benton, it would have been too much for them."

"Precisely. You did just enough. We have counselors who will now step in and talk with them. They will let us know when they are ready to work with us again. Enough for today. Take some time to rest and think about what you have been learning."

Several days passed before Naomi met with Sandrina

again. "I've spoken with the counselors," Sandrina began, "and I am told that Jensen and Benton are at a place where it would be safe for us to work with and open their Energies. Since my instructions are to teach you quite a bit within a short period of time, I will use this as an opportunity to teach you what two people can accomplish when they work together. Are you ready?"

"I suppose I am," Naomi said softly. "But I have no idea what you want me to do."

"Do you remember what you did when I asked you to work on Benton and Jensen's Energy the first time?"

"I guess so… No. I take that back. Actually, I don't. I remember meditating and focusing on them. Then I became calmer and I think I felt very centered. The next thing I knew it was over."

"Exactly. So don't worry. Just start by focusing into my Energy and we will go from there. Today we will take just a small step." She gave Naomi some brief instructions and then closed her eyes. Naomi closed her eyes as well. As she sensed Sandrina reaching out to her energetically, she felt herself being drawn into a peaceful, altered state. Beneath the surface, she could feel their union generating powerful currents of Energy. As instructed, she stayed detached from the buildup of Energy, allowing Sandrina to take the lead. Remaining passive and having only minimal conscious awareness of her surroundings, she had no idea of how much time passed before she felt herself returning to everyday consciousness. She felt clear, relaxed and - she noted with some surprise - extremely hungry.

"Good work, Sister Naomi. We have several hours before meeting with Jensen and Benton. Go get yourself some food and take a rest. You will find that you need both."

At the appointed hour, Naomi entered the Hall of Resolution and was surprised to encounter a smiling Jensen clapping Benton warmly on the back.

"Sorry, old buddy. I don't know why we didn't think of this before! My equipment is newer than yours, but you have some tools that I don't. So you're right. If we work the land together, we will get almost three times the yield. We can feed both our families with enough left over to make some profits." They looked up when Naomi and Sandrina entered the room. Benton spoke up. "I hope you accept our apologies for wasting your time. Turns out we didn't need your help. We worked it out ourselves. But we do want you to know we appreciate your trying. We're going to leave now so you can put your attention on those who really need you."

As they left the room, a smiling Sandrina winked at Naomi. "And that, my dear, is a demonstration of the power of opening Energies that are blocked."

Later that evening, Sandrina sat down with Naomi to review what she had been learning. "Tomorrow will be your last day of studying with me. Father Jerome wants you to return to the Inner Sanctum. There is one more thing I wish to show you, but now it is late. We shall meet tomorrow. Get a good night's rest tonight."

Naomi was surprised. "I won't be staying here to work with you?"

Sandrina looked equally surprised. "Is that what you really want?"

"I don't know," Naomi answered thoughtfully. "I'm not sure what I want - except maybe some clarification as to what I am meant to do."

"I think that is answer enough. You speak with doubt. My child, have faith. Some part of you knows that working here with me is not your path. When the time is right, you will be shown. Go now and get some sleep."

Chapter Fifteen

EARLY THE NEXT MORNING, Sandrina began working with Naomi. "Let me try to explain what we did yesterday. Basically, you entered an altered state through meditation which allowed me to access your Energy so that I could use it to augment my own. A passive person in that state can - shall we say -"lend" their Energy to another. However, even more can be accomplished when two people are actively working together. That is what we are going to try to do today. Understand, however, that there is not really very much I can tell you. Though we call it working together actively, it is really a process of deep surrender. Mostly you will have to find your own way. To begin, close your eyes and just focus on me in the same way you focused on Jensen and Benton. "

Naomi closed her eyes and felt the depth, calmness, and power that imbued Sandrina's Energy field. As she connected with her, she also felt the Energy begin to shift and realized that Sandrina was entering into a meditative trance state. Naomi's experiences had shown her that everyone held up protective walls and barriers. It was part of what made each person uniquely who they were. As Sandrina's state deepened, she could feel the boundaries eroding, taking Sandina into a state of connection with the "Infinite." Feeling Sandrina entering this state of ecstatic union, Naomi felt herself being drawn into the same state. At first it was exhilarating, but then it gradually became too much. Her sense of personal identity began to dissolve, and a part of her felt like she was dying. She pulled herself back abruptly.

"I'm sorry," Naomi said. "I don't know what happened. The fear became overwhelming and I had to break contact."

"It's OK. We may have tried this a bit too soon. Remember what happened when I worked with your Energy the other day?"

"Of course, how could I forget?"

Sandrina laughed. "No, that's not something one easily

forgets. We all have many such wounds contained within our Energy. The more of them we hold, the harder it is to open our field to working with another person. Certain wounds affect this kind of work more than others. Bathing in the sacred waters, as well as your Initiation Ceremony, have softened your blockages to engaging in this kind of teamwork. The ability to do so is there. It is similar to what you experienced during your Initiation when you felt connected to those of us around you. Yet, you also have resistance. People are multidimensional beings, and I sense that your blocks are not primarily from this immediate existence, but from traumas and experiences from other dimensions of your existence. I will talk to Father Jerome about this, but enough for now. For the present, my work with you is complete. Come, let's take a walk in the beautiful gardens and enjoy the rest of this day."

Chapter Sixteen

NOW, MAYBE I WILL finally know. Certainly Father Jerome will answer my questions today. I know I'm not supposed to keep looking ahead, but I'm just so curious... Naomi was so lost in her thoughts that she almost passed Father Jerome's office. She brought herself back to the present moment and knocked softly on his door.

"Enter," said the familiar voice. Opening the door, Naomi was surprised to see that Father Jerome was not alone. Seated across from him was an older man with wispy gray hair that looked like it was a stranger to the comb and had rarely encountered a barber. The man looked up when she entered, and she found herself looking into brown eyes that exuded such gentle kindness and compassion that she immediately felt her whole being relax. With her understanding of how Energies worked, she realized that this man would have a soothing effect on everyone he encountered.

"I was reading Sister Sandrina's report." Father Jerome's voice brought her back to the reason she was there. "It seems that you have learned quite a bit. You have seen how Energies can affect individuals; now it is time to learn how they affect groups. Father Daniel will be your mentor this time." He gestured toward the man sitting across from him. "This will require a bit of traveling for you. Go and prepare, as you will be leaving tomorrow. I will leave it to Father Daniel to explain the rest."

"But Father Jerome, I have several questions I would like to ask you before…"

"Yes, I am sure you do. But, the time is not yet ripe for answers. Patience, child. Everything in its time." Father Jerome turned to the man sitting across from him. "Father Daniel, do you have anything you would like to say at this point?"

Father Daniel focused his warm gaze in her direction. "You and I will have several days of traveling together - more than enough time for us to talk. I'm glad we had this moment to meet. I will look forward to seeing you in the morning."

And with that, the interview came to an end.

Chapter Seventeen

SEVERAL DAYS of traveling? Where could we possibly be going? I could go from one end of the country to the other in that time. She sighed loudly. She supposed that not knowing the answers was part of living simply, but it was disconcerting to have no control over what she did, where she went, and where her life was heading.

She met Father Daniel at the gate of the Temple. She tried to exude calm, but her face shone with excitement while her fluttery hands betrayed her nerves. This would be the first time she would leave the Temple grounds since her Initiation. "Ah, there you are," Father Daniel said cheerfully. "Well, our carriage is here. Are you ready? Once we are on board, I will explain our mission. Quite interesting, really, and not exactly an easy one."

From his chuckle, Naomi got the feeling that here was a man who enjoyed a good challenge. She wondered what he expected from her and what she was to learn from him. Why, she wondered, had she been sent from Sister Sandrina? Father Jerome said she had done a good job, but perhaps it had not been good enough. After all, her attempt to connect and work together actively with Sister Sandrina had been singularly unsuccessful due to her fear of letting go and surrendering. Maybe she had been sent to Father Daniel because he was good at difficult situations, and she would be another of his interesting challenges. Though she tried keeping her discouragement and insecurities at bay, she realized that they were feelings she had been dealing with repeatedly since first entering the Temple as a trainee.

"It will be good that we have so much time on our hands. There is so much to teach you," said Father Daniel. In her head, Naomi translated what she had heard to support her negative mood. She was the slow student who needed a lot more time than most. She sighed - something she was also doing quite often lately.

Three hours later Naomi's thoughts were spinning from trying to absorb all that she was hearing.

"You see, your theory about the importance of the Great Houses is entirely correct," Father Daniel continued, "when all work in harmony, the whole District benefits. Your own District is a wonderful example. The Great Houses work together more smoothly than in any other District. As a result, you have an almost nonexistent crime rate, a generally happy population, plus a high level of productivity and personal cooperation among your citizens. Energy starts at the top and works down. Heal those in leadership and the whole society begins to heal. Any healing always has a ripple effect. Heal any part of a group and the whole group benefits. Touch even one person and many will be touched by the results.

"Bringing this back to the task at hand, it means that in times of trouble, we don't have to resolve every conflict or heal every individual. We just have to make sure that those in power are ethical, govern fairly, and care about the people they are responsible for.

"Now, here's why our current assignment is so difficult. In our country, when a family in power abuses that power, we ask them to step down before the imbalance is out of control. The same is not true

of Pernandria - our eastern neighbor. They also use
ruling families working together to run Districts, but
have no way of removing a family that is not working
cooperatively for the good of their province. They now
have one District that has gotten dangerously out of
balance. Do you know that their citizens have actually
invented devices to put on their doors so that the doors
can only be opened by inserting a special long thin object
into them? They don't even trust their fellowmen to
refrain from entering their premises and taking what is
not theirs. Amazing, isn't it?

"Anyway, our task is to help restore balance. We have
sent teams to work on many fronts, but with little success.
We will be working on the level of Energy. It's really very
similar to what you did with Sandrina. We will just be doing
it on a larger scale by working to heal a group of people.
But then, if you think about it, groups are just made up of
multiple individuals.

"This will take more than just the two of us. We will be
met by three others who will work with us. You have always
been curious about the effects that Initiates could have on
society by working together. You are about to find out."

The rest of the trip flew by in animated discussion.

Father Daniel was right; clearly she had much to learn.

She looked forward to what the next day would bring.

Chapter Eighteen

"I'M EXHAUSTED. I must say I've never seen anything quite like it," Naomi said after a morning of meetings with Pernandrian ruling families. "Nobody listens to anyone else and they seem to care only about their own agendas. I don't see how we can make a difference here. They're all selfishly obsessed with what they consider to be success. How can they be willing to sacrifice the wellbeing of many just so that they can have more for themselves - and then consider that success? It makes absolutely no sense to me."

"It is rather exasperating," Father Daniel put in. He looked tired. "Our delegations have spent almost a year trying to show them the advantages of a society that takes care of all its people, but they have gotten nowhere.

I believe we are the last resort. I've never worked with such closed-minded people before. At least we now know what we're up against. Well, enough for today. The rest of our team has already arrived. Let's go meet them and fill them in."

Their quarters were in a separate building, and Father Daniel informed her that except for an occasional meeting, they and their team would remain apart from all others. They returned to meet with the new arrivals.

"Mother Cecelia and I have been working together for over twenty years now," Father Daniel said, starting the introductions. "Brother Felipe has worked with us for over seven years, and Brother Terrance is a relative newcomer - he joined us two years ago. I know you were all at her Initiation, but now I would like to personally introduce you to Naomi. She is just now learning what we do, but has not yet been able to actively link with others. She can, however, lend her Energies to the process. By the way, Naomi, among ourselves and after working together so long, we are quite informal here and just call each other by our names. You are one of us now and may join us in dispensing with the honorifics of Father, Mother, Brother or Sister."

Naomi awkwardly smiled at the group and shyly shook their hands as they were introduced. She knew nothing about them, yet was acutely aware of a sense of familiarity, like coming home to family. It was particularly strong when she made eye contact with Brother Terrance. For a moment she felt dizzy and disoriented. The room began to fade and she started to feel as though she was being transported to another time and space. She saw Terrance's face begin to morph - his nose widening and his skin darkening, and for a moment she thought she was surrounded by trees. The disorientation frightened her and she shook her head, reminding herself of where she was. The disconcerting visions faded.

Terrance smiled. "Don't be afraid of it. We inhabit multiple dimensions and know each other from many of them. You don't understand how to open yourself to them yet and fear losing the sense of self you most strongly identify with in this here and now. Regardless of that, I will say it's a pleasure to see you again and I look forward to 'reminiscing' about our times in those other dimensions. It is always a pleasure when we are together again. Welcome, dear one."

"Ahem," Father Daniel cleared his throat loudly. "I believe it is time we get to work. Let's begin by reviewing what we have learned and deciding upon a course of action."

As Daniel filled them in, they began discussing possible approaches.

Felipe animatedly paced back and forth as he shared his views, his thin wiry body emanating intensity and focused drive. "They have asked for our help and say they are willing to work with us, but are unwilling to make any personal changes or sacrifices. They seem to want us to magically make their society function better. They are not open to our mediators and won't acknowledge their individual responsibilities. They won't govern with integrity yet complain about crime and unfair business practices. No wonder so little has changed. Yes, we can work with them Energetically, since they have given us permission, but I don't think they are capable of consciously working with us in a cooperative manner. If we start unblocking them without being able to work with them afterwards, we could stir up more chaos than they are already experiencing."

"More than just chaos," Naomi added, remembering

her own experience of having her Energies opened. "Isn't it possible that we could precipitate mental or emotional breakdowns? Couldn't that be dangerous?"

"Yes, there could be some danger, but only if we go too fast. We would be sensitive to that and take it slowly. We have done this kind of work before, you know." Terrance smiled.

"Clearly, we have to take this one step at a time." Cecelia's voice was calm and clear as she outlined her ideas. "We know the importance of good leadership, and the Spinoza family is the family in charge. There is disharmony there and, of course, that filters down through the other families and to every rung of their society. Therefore, I suggest we start with the ruling family, and for now ignore everything and everyone else." A lively, yet totally harmonious discussion ensued, and within the hour they had agreed upon a plan. They would begin the next day.

Chapter Nineteen

"WE WON'T ASK you to work with us actively or even to lend your Energies at this point," Daniel said. "Father Jerome told me about your experiences with Sandrina. We have agreed that you are not yet ready, but you can learn by observing. Cecelia, Felipe and I will link our energies, while Terrance explains to you what is going on. You will see that several of us working together can accomplish more than a single individual.

Cecelia, Felipe and Daniel sat in a small circle in the middle of the floor. After briefly making eye contact, they closed their eyes and entered into a meditative state.

"There's really not much to see, but pay attention to what you feel. If you open yourself to it, you can sense quite a bit," Terrance commented. "For now, just notice how relaxed and comfortable they all are."

Daniel sat straight, his body almost unnaturally still, yet looking completely at ease. Felipe's intensity was palpable even with his eyes closed and his body relaxed, while Cecelia's face glowed with a beautiful inner radiance. Mesmerized, Naomi felt herself being drawn into their peaceful stillness. As time went on, their Energies seemed to merge, each contributing a bit of themselves to make a greater whole. Daniel was the core and foundation. His stability was energized by Felipe's intensity, while he reciprocally smoothed out some of Felipe's driving passions. Cecelia softened both of them and expanded their Energies, enabling all three of them to reach greater depth of meditation and heights of spiritual connection. Cecelia then used their increased strength and deepened connection to augment her own abilities. Naomi observed the Energies continue to shift and merge until she could no longer tell where one ended and another started. She was enthralled, but for some reason it also made her uncomfortable.

"Why does it frighten you so?" Terrance asked gently. "When we blend that way, we become as one. There is no sense of individual identity, but afterwards we always return to ourselves. It takes a skilled leader to guide us, and Daniel is one of the best. The process takes trust - in yourself as well as the others. At your deepest level of awareness you sense you can trust us; it appears to be yourself that you question. You will need to face your fears before you can work with us. You have been wondering about your place in the Temple. Here is your answer. Father Jerome tells us that you are meant for this work and that you will, in time, join our group. It is a great honor. Few are able to do what is required, and even fewer are chosen."

As soon as she heard this, her heart sang with joy. Everything began to make sense - including her dreams about the orbs floating in space. These magnificent people were the orbs calling to her to join them, and it was her terror of letting go, of losing her individual identity and being consumed by the Energies of the group, that blocked her. "How will I overcome my fear? I don't even understand what it is about."

"Don't worry yourself. I have no doubt that Daniel will find a way and the rest of us will help. Be patient. Everything happens in its own perfect time. It's not yet happening, so obviously it's not yet time." Terrance's smile reached into the core of her being and began to awaken deeply buried feelings and stirrings of what felt like an ancient awareness. Once again, he seemed to sense what was inside of her.

"Naomi, we travel together in many dimensions, and my presence awakens your awareness of other times and places. Always it is so when people's souls are so deeply entwined. The majority of people are mostly asleep, so they fail to recognize the significance. They merely register that they like someone, dislike someone, or feel comfortable or uncomfortable around someone. They are oblivious to the rest. You are on the cusp of awakening, so you recognize me but are still too afraid of losing the identity you currently cling to. Therefore, you won't allow yourself to merge with other dimensions and truly remember who you are." His awareness shifted and he glanced at the three sitting in the middle. "They will be finishing soon. See what you can sense."

The center of the room felt like a ball of healing light. As Naomi observed, she felt the intensity dim and slowly differentiate into three smaller balls of light. Slowly, these also dimmed and suddenly she could once again sense three discrete personalities. As they opened their eyes, they all looked radiant and refreshed. They checked in with each other through their eyes, each breaking contact after a brief nod. It was over, and the room returned to its previous Energetic state.

Cecelia was the first to speak. "It is a start and a good one. I don't believe we can do any more yet. Let's wait a few days, then check to see if there are any repercussions. If all goes well, we can take another step very soon. My guess is that we won't see any results for a few weeks, and nothing significant for a few months. We'll just take it slowly. Now, how about some food?"

The others nodded in agreement.

The more Naomi learned, the more she longed to be able to work actively with the other Initiates. Though she was able to lend her Energies, she was still unable to completely surrender. The others remained supportive and counseled patience.

Chapter Twenty

NAOMI WAS NO LONGER surprised by the power of Energy to change people. Three months after their work began, the Spinoza family - the family that ruled Pernandria - seemed to have mysteriously developed more compassion, both in their dealings with one another and with the other ruling families. She watched with fascination as the society began to slowly heal. Sharing became a higher value than hoarding, and the good of the many took precedence over the comfort of the few.

Daniel explained how it worked. "You see, man is basically good but also inherently self-centered. At our best, we are righteous, generous and willing to be there for our fellow man. But life is also challenging. When we are hurt, feel threatened, disappointed, or thwarted in getting what we want, we can be deterred from our nobler instincts and become petty, selfish, and even cruel. These negative states of mind create the blockages you have learned to feel in people's Energies. When we remove these blocks, a person may have a difficult time - as you did when Sandrina opened your Energy. However, the more the blocks are removed, the more people's basic goodness shines forth. We have done all that we can at this point. Goodness begets goodness, and now the process can slowly continue to unfold on its own. It's time to return to the Temple."

Chapter Twenty-One

"SO, DO WE HAVE a special title? What is our primary purpose?" Having returned to the Temple and residing once again in the Inner Sanctum, Naomi seemed to have an endless stream of questions. Luckily, Father Jerome seemed to have an equally endless well of patience.

"No, we don't have a special title and most people are not even aware of our existence. Not even many Initiates know that there is a community of Healers living here in the Inner Sanctum. As you know, most Initiates come to the Inner Sanctum only for their Initiation. They enter, go directly to the Hall of Initiation, receive their Initiation and then leave, never to return.

"Many of us who live here never leave the Inner Sanctum. Those who do leave usually do so only to work in the Temple - or on rare occasions to perform a healing service - like when you traveled to Pernandria.

"As for our purpose, we generate and direct healing flows of Light Energy. When we link up, we form a circle of light that radiates out like the ripple in a pond when you toss in a pebble. As you have surmised, by doing so we use the power to affect society as a whole. This would be difficult for you to comprehend had you not seen the power of Energies to change people. You have seen it work with individuals and small groups. We do the same thing for larger groups - much larger groups."

"It all sounds wonderful," Naomi sighed. "Will I ever be able to surrender and work actively with my group? Everyone tells me to be patient, but I'm getting discouraged."

"You must learn to trust that everything happens in its own perfect time." Father Jerome chided. "I can assure you that you don't have much longer to wait. Come to the Hall of Initiation an hour before sunrise on the day of the full moon, two days hence. We will see what we can do. You will be fine, child. Don't worry. Go now. It's time for dinner." As Naomi left the room her thoughts were charged with curious excitement about what would happen in two days' time.

Chapter Twenty-Two

THE WARM GLOW of the full moon shed just enough illumination to light her way to the Hall of Initiation. She was not the first to arrive. Daniel greeted her, took her hand and led her inside the building. "Sit here. The others are arriving and we will begin as the sun rises." He pointed to the intricately laid mosaic pattern she had sat upon during her Initiation.

The room was no less awe-inspiring by moonlight. She sensed the powerful Energies that inhabited the space and felt her consciousness expand in their presence. Without effort or intent, she entered an altered state of consciousness. The Energies shifted and her state deepened as the others arrived. It was time. They were all here as they had been during her Initiation. She knew this but felt no need to question how she knew. A part of her asked, *Time for what?* The question faded. It had no relevance. The one Naomi knew as Daniel greeted her. Naomi. That label seemed unimportant, as did the label Daniel. What difference did these names really make? Daniel, Douglas Fairway, Gandje - they were all one and the same and yet not the same. "Let these thoughts go," an unidentified voice spoke directly within her mind. "They have no place here. Don't try to order the experience. It need not make sense. Go where you are led. Let go of Naomi."

She surrendered.

Expansion…Light…Images…Disparate parts… A longing to be whole…Sharp pain of wounds…Tears… Unbearable longing…Understanding…The wounds keep the wholeness at bay…Sorrow…Loneliness…such profound loneliness…Rivers of tears…

"You are not alone, child. Follow the wounds. Heal them."

"Gandje? Are you here with me?"

"Yes, child. Journey to the life in which you name me as Gandje. Many answers lie there."

She found herself in a peaceful village. She was a

happy child. She gazed at her mother and her heart swelled with joy and love.

"NO!" she screamed. "Don't take her away. I need her!" But she could do nothing, for in the soul of her mother was a disease that would end her brief sojourn in that particular form. Her mother's spirit tried to reach her. "Dearest, this is a continuous journey that we circle in many forms. I will leave you here, but am never truly gone. I love you with all my heart. Please understand that this is a journey our souls require. The cycle will end as soon as you realize wholeness. I promise you this."

But the one known as Nadjia could not hear, for her tears closed her heart to the voice. The spirit left her mother's body. The child's spirit broke. She was a magnificent child, for the Spirit within her was strong. But the Child of Spirit was wounded by the loss of the mother, and this weakened her and made her fragile. On the surface all seemed fine, and might have continued that way, but her tests were to be many. Her destiny needed her to be resilient, with a strength forged in the fires of adversity. It mattered not how long it took or how many wounds she might endure. Nothing would be considered a failure - all was only growth and experience

- steady growth toward her destiny.

Naomi remained a passive observer as Nadjia's life continued to unfold. She watched Nadjia mature into a beautiful young woman, fall in love, and become betrothed. From Naomi's vantage point, she could sense the frailty within Nadjia's psyche that was invisible to those around her. Gandje, in his role as Tribal Father, had filled the emptiness left by the loss of her father. However, the wound from the loss of Nadjia's mother was deepened by the coldness and disapproval of her Aunt Damaya. She witnessed Damaya's betrayal and saw Nadjia being thrown into a dark locked cell. And at that moment, she saw Nadjia's spirit falter and nearly break.

She felt a flash of hatred toward Damaya. *You were meant to protect her - not weaken her! How could you!*

"Shush, child." She felt Cecelia's sweet compassion communicate these words to her mind. "All is as it should be. Many are the journeys a soul must make to reach wholeness. Look more closely at the one you name Damaya. What do you see?"

She looked again and was surprised. The one called Damaya also carried the name Sarita - her beloved nursemaid. *How? Sarita is nothing like Damaya!* she thought. She sensed another voice - this one she recognized as Daniel's. "There would be no growth if an experience endlessly repeated. We must learn all sides. This soul in the form of Damaya had much to learn; as Sarita, she has regained both balance and the ability to love. In this existence as Sarita, she has protected you and tried to lovingly fill the void left by the loss of your mother. Her soul has now healed and will no longer need to recreate this particular lesson."

Naomi's heart opened with compassion for the one called Damaya, and her anger dissolved. Still, other wounds gaped, demanding attention and veiling wholeness. She observed this self that was her but not her. The darkness of the cell that Nadjia had been thrown into reflected a growing darkness within Nadjia's spirit. The feelings of abandonment she had kept at bay with the death of her father and mother surfaced as she sat alone and afraid in the dark cell. Fear radiated outward, and Nadjia's trusting connection to her spirit weakened.

"This is the first wound that keeps you from connection," Daniel's voice spoke into her mind. "Explore it. As each aspect of your soul heals, all other aspects heal as well. You have arrived at a point in your development where you can reach out from your soul and heal the wounds from all dimensions of experience. See the parts knit together as a whole. You are a healer, but the first person you must heal is yourself."

She returned to the searing pain of terror and abandonment and felt Nadjia's tender young soul contracting and withering. Consumed with helplessness, Naomi reached out with her mind for help. "What can I do? How can I help?"

Cecelia's soothing vibration responded, "Know who you are, Naomi. Know yourself for the bright Light and Healer that is the essence of your being. Feel your strength. Trust your knowledge. Center yourself and come from a place of Love. We are all here with you and are all helping. Feel our presence; we give you added strength."

Naomi's soul responded, and something within her awoke. *Yes, she thought, I can do this - we can do this. Nadjia is also myself. We need each other and must work together so that once again we become as one.* Reaching within to the depths of her power, she radiated love and light from that center. The part of her that was Nadjia sensed her presence. An aspect of herself that felt old and wise spoke to the part that seemed young and innocent.

Naomi spoke to Nadjia. "Greetings, Dear One. Sometimes adversity is our greatest teacher. Be not afraid, for out of the deepest dark comes the greatest illumination. In this time of stillness and emptiness you can truly know this. If only I could show you, but alas there is no way. Find me inside of you, for that is where I abide. Feel the peace that comes of our union. Know that you are never truly alone. Know your power. Trust your gifts. Your soul is the soul of a healer and a knower. Always has it been so. Always will it be so. Remember, I am with you always."

Nadjia, not knowing that Naomi was an aspect of her own being, saw her as a separate entity and called her "Being of Light." Nadjia's connection to her soul was restored and she was now filled with peace. But a frailty remained at her core, so Naomi stayed with her and followed her as her life unfolded, lending her strength and keeping her from feeling alone and abandoned. She felt Nadjia's courage, her deep trust of all that was spiritual, and her acceptance of fate, and Naomi made that courage and trust and acceptance her own. She felt Nadjia's heart ache for the one she loved, and Naomi recognized that the same ache lived in her own psyche. The same longing consumed her.

"Nadjia and Naomi are one, not two. Her wounds are yours. Heal them for both of you. Remember who you are, Dear One. Twin Souls are always happiest when reunited, but you cannot fully love until you recognize your wholeness. When you are whole you will remember. When you remember, the gifts will be many." The voice soothed her heart. "Her fear still lives within you, and has made you incapable of surrendering to Love. Love has myriad expressions. When we link together in our healing circle, we do so in Love. When you learn to Love, you will be able to surrender and actively work with us."

Naomi stayed by Nadjia's side and watched over her. What an amazing circle of life! Naomi was healing herself in another dimension while also learning about simplicity and faith from this seemingly more primitive expression of herself. Simultaneously, much of the strength of Nadjia's faith came from her trust in what she called the Being of Light - what some might term a "later" incarnation of her own soul. The cycle was beautiful in its perfection.

She studied Nadjia's life, looking for the key to healing both of their heartaches. Nadjia had lost her parents and been ripped away from her tribe. Her soul carried a deep wound of abandonment. She therefore felt her separation from Nardjol, her betrothed, as further abandonment. In her darker moments, she pictured him blissfully married to another, having completely forgotten her. These thoughts were too painful to bear, and were always brushed quickly aside, but the wound remained. Sometimes Nadjia worried that the Being of Light would also abandon her. Naomi did what she could to reassure her, but her ability to communicate with her directly was limited.

Naomi reached out once again for help. "I remain at her side and will not abandon her. She is learning to trust me, but it is her beloved she longs for, and this longing wounds her all the more."

"Then seek out her beloved," came the reply.

"But how?"

"We are all here. We lend you our strength and our support, but you must find your own way." This came from many voices. They blended together and she could no longer identify them individually. She strengthened herself by joining more closely with their Energies, the boundaries between them becoming blurred.

She reached out to Nardjol, Nadjia's beloved. She could sense him, but only dimly.

"He is not another aspect of yourself. You will need our help to reach him. Connect with us; use our combined strength." Without thought, she moved past her fear and further strengthened her connection to the group.

Nardjol's longing for Nadjia was as strong as Nadjia's longing for Nardjol. He searched for her in vain, willing to risk all to find her. She observed helplessly. "Look deeper," the voices intoned in her mind. "Let go of all preconceptions. Release your fears. Open your heart. What do you see?"

Why did Naomi fear connecting to Nardjol? She opened wider. The aching in her heart grew stronger. She despaired in her loneliness, but was afraid of uniting. Connection was too painful - it always ended in abandonment. The perceived boundaries softened between Naomi and Nadjia. Nadjia had lost her mother, her beloved, her tribe, her way of life. Naomi felt tears streaming down her own face. She grieved the loss of her own mother, her current separation from her father, her inability to love David, her fear of opening to actively working with the group, her fear of surrendering to Love. The tears abated, her spirit calmed. She recognized familiarity, and her heart expanded. "Terrance?" She reached out to identify his spirit. "You and Nardjol are one. You are the one she longs for - the one we both long for." Long-buried feelings swirled and rose to the surface. "That is why I feel the way I do around you. I have denied the feelings because they frightened me. I am sorry." This time the tears were tears of joy.

"Yes, beloved. In this dimension we are reunited. Now that you recognize me, open your heart to me so that we can work together. I can reach Nardjol as you can reach Nadjia. They have work to do in their dimension, just as we have work to do in ours."

Naomi could still not completely surrender, but she and Terrance worked together with the support of the others. She protected Nadjia and helped keep her spirit and faith strong. Terrance guided Nardjol in sacred rituals in order to help him find his way back to Nadjia. Years passed for Nadjia and Nardjol, but time had no meaning in the dimension that Naomi and Terrance inhabited. Pain and disappointment were frequent companions to Nadjia and Nardjol. Naomi and Terrance were only aware of the growth and healing of their spirits. What did a moment of pain matter in the grander scheme of a soul awakening?

At last the moment arrived, and at the sacred site of their old village they were once again in each other's arms, where they belonged. Naomi radiated with delight. She and Terrance had worked together to realize wholeness and harmony. This part of her task was complete. She felt Terrance reach out to her mind. "Come, Dear One. We must return now. This work is taxing and we are all nearing our limit. Food and rest await us."

Naomi returned. Aware only of confusion and disorientation, she tried to make sense of her surroundings. Why was she in the Hall of Initiation? Images and memories wafted through her mind but were too fleeting for her to grasp. She tried to stand but was overcome with weakness. The world started to spin and she felt strong arms catch her as she began to faint.

She slept for eighteen hours, woke up long enough to eat, and then promptly fell back asleep. On the morning of the third day she awoke, stretched, and finally felt aware of more than hunger and a fuzzy feeling

in her brain. Images and memories began to flood
her consciousness. She remained still, her eyes closed,
absorbing and integrating all that she had experienced,
knowing she would never be the same. Hearing a
movement in the room, her eyes flew open and she found
herself face to face with Terrance. He had stayed by her
side, waiting for her to awaken. At first she felt shy and
awkward, but gazing into his eyes left her with a feeling
of familiar comfort. She was home. This was family.
True, she knew very little of Terrance in this dimension,
but their souls had journeyed together so many times
that this was of little importance. They were friends and
lovers, who had been apart for a seeming interval of time
but were now reunited. They spent the next several days
filling in the details of their "time apart".

She met again with Father Jerome and Father Daniel.
There was much to share and much more to learn. Pleased
with Naomi's progress, they agreed to schedule another
ritual in the Hall of Initiation at the next full moon.

As usual, Naomi was told nothing of what to expect -
only that there was more healing to take place.

Chapter Twenty-Three

SHE HAD BEEN told to let go of expectations and just be open, yet her mind kept drifting back to the last time she had been in the Hall of Initiation. Would it be as powerful and transformative this time? She sat upon the mosaic pattern in the floor of the Hall of Initiation and waited for something magical and mystical to take place. The light shifted. Sunrise was at hand, yet nothing was happening. She began to fret. Maybe not everyone was here; perhaps that was the trigger that started everything off. She had a vague recollection that last time she somehow knew without being told when all were present. Now, she felt nothing.

"Naomi." She heard Daniel's voice. He was speaking aloud, not in her mind as had happened last time. "You're trying too hard to make something happen. Nothing will happen if you lead with your mind. Stop your worries, your thoughts and your expectations. Allow the experience to unfold."

He was right. Last time she had just opened herself to the Energies in the room. This time she was trying to figure out what was expected of her and how to proceed. Closing her eyes, she opened her being. Her consciousness expanded, leaving her feeling less connected to her physical form. She reacted with anxiety.

"Explore the anxiety. It is part of what keeps you from surrendering. Don't be afraid. As always, we will be right here with you." The voices were reassuring. She stretched her awareness toward the anxiety and felt herself drifting into another state of being. She was not prepared for what she experienced.

—∿—

She saw the lights of the oncoming car and realized with horror that it was coming directly at them. It happened so fast. There was no time for thought as she felt the car hurtling down the steep ravine. Her next awareness was of someone lying on the ground, his leg bent at an unnatural angle and blood streaming out of his stomach. She didn't realize that anything was amiss until she reached out to help him and discovered that she couldn't make physical contact with him. That was when she realized she was no longer in a physical body. Her first response was terror. There was only one possible interpretation. She must be dead. She had never before felt so terrified…

—∽—

Naomi pulled herself back from the image, her heart pounding and her body covered in sweat. This was nothing like what she had experienced the last time she was in the Hall of Initiation. The experience was so much more intense and more terrifying. She couldn't breathe. She wanted it all to stop - no way was she going back there.

She heard them speaking to her in her mind. "You must help her. Though for this moment we speak of her as a separate being, she is another aspect of yourself. What happened should not have happened. In that dimension, she lacks the training and experience to understand what has taken place. Because of the depth of her/your soul's spiritual connection, an accident that would have rendered most people temporarily unconscious has thrown her out of her physical body. She is not prepared to deal with this. She is not dead and is still connected to her physical form. If her panic does not subside soon, her physical heart will fail and she will die. This fear has left its mark on your soul. She is trapped in an alternate dimension, and you as Naomi are the only one who can reach her. Until the terror that attends this experience is overcome and the lessons learned, you will panic each time you come close to transcending the limitations of your physical form. This challenge and lesson will repeat in different ways until you master it. Each deep wound of the soul must be healed in order to discover wholeness. And this wound is quite deep, as you can see from the terror you are feeling here and now. Go back. You must help. In that dimension you must first overcome the fear of operating independently, outside the physical body. Once that is accomplished, the foundation for rediscovering your gifts as a healer will be set. Remember, the more our soul advances, the closer we become to remembering our Oneness, and the more each aspect of our self can heal other aspects.

"The one known then as Brian, is supplying the opportunity to learn valuable lessons through his experience of being injured. Currently you know that same soul as David - and once again he has indirectly helped you realize your soul's purpose." Naomi took some time to absorb this new information and to center herself before attempting to return.

Perhaps her decision was based on fear of revisiting the scene of terror. Whatever the reason, Naomi decided to return to an earlier time before the accident to learn more about this aspect of her soul. She discovered that in this life her name was Alicia and that she was a doctor. She was intrigued to learn that she did not lose her mother this time, but that her mother had been a cold, distant figure who failed to provide maternal nurturance. Another "mother wound," but this time from maternal neglect rather than absence.

Slowly, Naomi returned to the accident scene and tried making a connection with the terrified Alicia. It was difficult since Alicia was much less spiritually sensitive than Nadjia. Naomi settled for sending soothing vibrations and trying to influence Alicia's consciousness with Energetic reassurances and subtle guidance. As she had done with Nadjia, Naomi stayed with Alicia. She sought openings to help her, but was at a loss as to what else she could do. Naomi reached out to the group, asking for assistance.

"Alicia is not very open and you are not strong enough to reach her very effectively on your own," they responded. "You can direct the Energy of the group, enabling us to connect with her together. It will be difficult and exhausting for you to speak to her on your own. You can, however, continue to send her support and Energy. You cannot do anything directly unless she asks. Do everything you can to find ways to encourage Alicia to ask for help. Look for people around Alicia who are more open. Sometimes it is possible to give suggestions through other people. Look for openings and you will find them."

Naomi found a doctor who was sensitive to other dimensions and stuck close by him. He was clearly aware of Alicia's presence outside of her body, yet seemed unaware of Naomi's presence as well. Still, Naomi hoped she could encourage him to get Alicia to ask for help. Unsure if she had succeeded or if he just intuitively knew what to tell Alicia, she was nonetheless overjoyed when she saw him directing his words to the exact spot on the ceiling where Alicia's disembodied spirit was hovering.

Naomi heard him tell Alicia that the man who had been in the car with her needed some help, and Naomi was ecstatic when she heard him say:

"It's just a question of learning what must be done. If I didn't know what to do, personally I'd ask for assistance. Never know what kind of help is out there - if you know what I mean. No good trying to do it all alone, but sometimes people are afraid to ask for help. Yup, I know how this stuff works. Asking for help - that's the ticket."

Finally, Alicia asked for help. Now the problem was how to supply that help. Naomi needed the added strength of the group. Considering how scared Alicia was of what she might encounter, they decided to approach her in the least threatening form they could come up with - that of an angel.

Gathering the Energies of the group, she formed a strong circle of white light and shaped it into the form of an angel. And in a beautiful blend of voices, they began to speak.

"Greetings, Alicia. You have asked for our help."

Naomi was a bit disappointed with Alicia's response

to the angelic presence: "You've got to be kidding! I can't believe this. I mean…Are you for real? Like, you guys really exist?"

Naomi thought she'd better try something else. She dissolved the angel and instead formed the image of an Oriental-looking man in a monk's robe and with wise kind eyes. "Does this form make you more comfortable? You did ask that our appearance not frighten you. Is there another form you would prefer?"

Alicia's response to this form was more accepting. "No, I guess you made your point. You can be whatever I want you to be and if I'm frightened, it's my own choice to feel so. This form is as good as any."

They had made contact. Naomi could feel how much energy it was taking to sustain such direct contact, and she knew they would not be able to speak for long. Once again, she directed the Energy of the group.

"We don't need to be in any form at all. We can speak directly to your consciousness, but we determined that doing so would make you uncomfortable; we will, therefore, remain in a form that exists as separate from yourself. We are limited in what we can do. We have heard your request. We cannot heal Brian directly, nor can we impart knowledge to you directly. We can offer you what you need, but it will be up to you to make sense of it all. Listen carefully. Here is our gift to you. You sensed correctly. What is wrong with Brian is an echo from the past. Follow the echo and heal the wound. Doing so will heal you as well."

Naomi focused her power, desperately needing to say something directly to this alternate aspect of her Self.

"Right now, it's not possible for me to say or do more. However, I will be with you, helping and supporting you in every way I can. Don't be afraid. All will be well. Listen to the silence within, for that is where I will be. Farewell. Remember, you are not alone."

Her Energy dwindled, and her ability to maintain contact was lost.

Naomi felt the support of the group around her. "You have done enough and have given her what she needs. She will now overcome her fear. You have forged a bond and she can connect to you when she needs assistance. You must return now. We are all reaching our limit and the work has taxed you greatly. To stay here longer would be dangerous. She will find her way and you will both reap the benefits. These two aspects of yourself will now both become more integrated."

This time, Naomi was prepared for the disorientation and exhaustion she felt upon completing the ritual.

Chapter Twenty-Four

"WHY ARE YOU so discouraged? You can do much more than you could before, including surrendering when we work in smaller groups." Terrance was holding her hand as they walked through the beautiful gardens.

"But the most powerful healing work occurs when the entire group works as one. Daniel tells me that the groups are made up of souls with strong karmic connections, and that you have been waiting for me to join you, but I'm not sure that I can ever completely surrender. Sure, I do fine now with one or two others, but I never completely lose awareness of myself, and am therefore the weak link in any healing work we do. I was so exhausted after the last ritual that I'm not even allowed to participate in another one for three whole months. Oh,

Terrance. What if I can't break through? Maybe I'm just not strong enough for this work."

"Patience, dear one. You're the only one who has any doubts. You'll see. There are many reasons to wait before doing another ritual. One is that you need time to recuperate and to further strengthen yourself, but you also need time to integrate all that you have experienced and all that you have learned. Each experience has been profound and deeply transformative - changing you down to your core. The three months will seem to go by much faster if you relax, accept what is, and allow yourself to enjoy them."

—⁓—

Three months later when it was time to meet again in the Hall of Initiation, a more relaxed and confident Naomi was ready. Only nine other Initiates had attended the last two rituals; this time all twelve were there. The additional Initiates were the three women who had been her guides on the day of her Initiation. Jenny and Paulina were the younger guides, and she had spent many an hour with them. However, she never had the opportunity to spend time with Bea, the older guide.

This would be the first time Naomi would work with her group in its entirety. When it was time to begin, she felt her consciousness shift, and was aware of the love and support of the others. "Blend with our Energies," the voices urged, reaching out to her. "When you feel resistance, explore it." There was no fear this time, no pain, but connection with the others was difficult. She slipped into sadness. She didn't belong here. She didn't belong anywhere. She was alone and separate. Loneliness was something she had to endure; there was no other way.

"Blend with us. We are here."

No, that was for other people - people who had families, people who had mothers. Her path was one that had to be walked alone. Otherwise, she would have known the sweet confidence of a mother's love, not the devastating upheaval of its loss. This wound had occurred too many times. Nothing was worth the risk of reawakening the pain. She would be content as she was. She pushed the voices away and retreated to a space of silence and peace. But the loneliness grew. She reminded herself that she had managed to survive without a mother; she could, therefore, survive without anyone close to her. Her heart betrayed her by longing for its twin - its mate of the soul. A name formed and then blended with other names - Terrance, Nardjol, Christopher, Blakely… myriad forms of the same soul. Longing grew and she longed to reach out, but… No! That was for other people. Hers was a solitary path. Naomi's heart wept.

"You are not alone. Open your heart. Feel the thread of love. Follow it. Love can come in many forms. You are dearly loved."

She heard their voices, but they seemed far away. She felt the thread and longed to follow it. No. That was for other people. People who belonged - it was not meant for her. She closed herself off from the voices and returned to the silence. She closed her heart. But one thin thread persisted. It tugged on her and would not let go. Reluctantly, she followed it…

Nadjia was such a happy child - filled with love and grace. She adored her mother and felt such joy in her presence…

No. I must not go back there. I know where that leads. That kind of joy can't last. Enduring joy is for others. I must stand alone. The thread pulled at her again - pulled and pulled and would not stop. A voice tried to speak with her, but she pushed it away. It tried again, and this time she caught a whisper of its message. "Go back. A mother's love can come in many forms. This soul as Nadjia's mother presents you with a gift. She did not abandon you. You needed to learn to stand apart, not to reject being together. A soul that cannot stand alone has naught to give to others. You learned that lesson - maybe too well. Now learn that a soul that cannot open to others also has nothing to give. Heal the wound."

The message shifted, becoming more personal. "Dearest, listen. I too have been left wounded. We need to heal. I am sorry that my leaving brought you such pain. It has brought me equal pain. Come, child. Let us heal."

"Mother?"

"Yes, child. The wound is strongest when you experience life as Nadjia. Explore it. I am here, but first you must heal the wound there."

She returned and opened her heart to the mother. Pain and bliss beyond imagining. Tears of loss, mingled with tears of joy. Recognition and awe for the wondrous, complex fabric of existence. As her heart expanded she recognized this soul - the mother of Nadjia was present here and now in the form of Bea, the older woman guide.

An awareness brushed her consciousness but was lost in the waves of emotion that swept through her. She rode the waves, buffeted by sensations and feelings, almost drowning in their intensity. When she could take no more, she crashed into the metaphorical shore, feeling solid ground once more beneath her - and she lay in a stupor.

"There is more," the voice suggested - but she could take no more. Again she retreated into the silence of separateness. Eons passed - or maybe just moments. Time had no meaning in this dimension. The tempest passed. She peered out from her fortress of solitude.

"There is more when you are ready." The voice had not given up. It had not left her. She felt comforted.

There was something more to see - something to do with here and now - something to do with Mother - something to do with Bea. Something to do with her name. Her name…And then it came to her. Bea - short for Bethany. Her mother had never died! She saw the scene unfold in her mind - her mother's spiritual awakening and her need to enter the Temple and become an Initiate; their souls once again having to experience separation. It was a dance they had shared over and over again - whether through death or separation. And it was time for that dance to end. No longer did the soul of her mother need to learn the lessons of leaving a child behind, and no longer did Naomi have to live with the painful emptiness caused by losing her mother. Learning what was needed, each had become stronger. It was time for them to join together and heal. Bethany, her mother, now came to her, sitting beside her on the mosaic pattern in the center of the Hall of Initiation. No longer in trance, they fell into each other's arms and wept until there were no more tears to weep. The others filed out slowly and quietly, knowing this would take quite some time.

Chapter Twenty-Five

SHE WAS WHOLE - at last - having knit together
and integrated the separate aspects of her soul. She
had faced her worst fears, and her wounds had healed,
allowing her to walk through life with a surety and
a fullness that was different from anything she had
previously known. Her vision was unlike the perceptions
of those who had not experienced unity with the
soul. It was more than knowing that everything was
interconnected; it was being able to "see" and experience
the connections. She could "see" how every prior
experience had led her to this moment - the painful ones
as well as the joyful ones, the moments of feeling lost and
confused along with the moments of crystal clarity. Every
moment and every experience was perfect.

The present ceremony was at an end. Having experienced the bliss of surrendering and connecting with the others, she felt serene and fulfilled. They had been as one, but now each returned to his or her individual identity. Making eye contact, she nodded to each one, acknowledging their divine grace and their individuality. This helped her to gradually return to her own small identity as Naomi. She smiled at her mother. In her present state, it seemed absurd and even amusing that she had ever thought herself separated from her. But then much of her understanding of the world was different when she was in conscious connection with her soul.

How strange, she thought. As a group, we gather and direct powerful healing forces, yet almost no one knows what we do or that we even exist. In the Temple, we live apart from the world, staying within the Inner Sanctum. Yet the world is a better place for our efforts.

Once she had been accused of running away from the world by going to live in the Temple. But she had not turned away from the world, just from the illusions that blinded most people. Now she understood. Illusions, caused by perceiving only a part of the whole, were the source of all pain, fear, confusion, anger, and doubt.

Before, she had been blinded by fear and ignorance. Now, she could see clearly. Now she knew that there is only Light and Love. Now she knew that everything and everyone is intertwined - even time itself. By healing the multiple facets of her soul, she had reached her destiny, taking her place as a Healer of Mankind. She felt a presence by her side, and a familiar hand reached out to take hers. She smiled at Terrance as they walked from the Hall of Initiation.